Ann Summers

True Stories as Told to Madame B

Ann Summers

True Stories as Told to Madame B

EBURY
PRESS

3 5 7 9 10 8 6 4 2

Published in 2007 by Ebury Press, an imprint of Ebury Publishing

Ebury Publishing is a division of the Random House Group

Text written by Siobhan Kelly © Ebury Press 2007

The Random House Group Limited Reg. No. 954009

Addresses for companies within the Random House Group can be found at
www.randomhouse.co.uk

A CIP catalogue record for this book
is available from the British Library

The Random House Group Limited makes every effort to ensure that
the papers used in our books are made from trees that have been
legally sourced from well-managed and credibly certified forests. Our
paper procurement policy can be found on www.randomhouse.co.uk

Printed in the UK by CPI Cox & Wyman, Reading, RG1 8EX

ISBN: 9780091916459

CONTENTS

FOREWORD

Welcome to Ann Summers' new collection of erotic short stories, a new and thrilling series destined to become essential bedtime reading.

I'm really excited to be able to bring you these ten tales of women who boldly go wherever their desires take them. We know that our customers are the sexually confident, fabulous women who love sex and aren't afraid to show it.

From the no-holds-barred stories to the gentle and romantic, I promise that this collection of erotic tales has something for each and every one of you. So without any further ado, I hand you over to our narrator, the mysterious Madame B . . .

Jacqueline Gold

Welcome to a collection of tales to titillate and tease, awaken and arouse you.

My name is Madame B, and I am a collector. I collect other women's sexual confessions: true stories from women who took a walk on the sexual wild side, and decided to share their sizzling secrets with me.

My job involves travelling the world and meeting new and remarkable ladies every day. In my experience, all women have at least one sexual confession, ranging from extreme tales of exhibitionism to the memory of a stolen kiss that still induces a shiver down the spine years later. And you'd be surprised how eager they are to share these stories with me.

Some of these confessions have been told to me in far-flung bars, others over coffee in my local café. Some women write letters to me detailing their exploits: others prefer to email or phone. I write all the confessions down in a red-leather notebook that lives beside my bed. Some stories are so sexually charged that I'm ready to climax after transcribing the first few lines: others are subtle slow-burners that take two or three reads to unveil the full extent of their sexual power.

And now I've assembled so many confessions that my little red book is nearly full. It seems a shame not to share the cream of my collection with a wider audience. So here is my choice of the most orgasmic, arousing confessions I've ever heard. The women who spill their secrets to me come from all walks of life but they all have one thing in common: they've taken their sexual fantasies to the limit and fulfilled their orgasmic potential. Some of their stories are soft and romantic; some are shocking and hardcore. Most are a combination of the two. None of them are politically correct. All of them really happened.

I hope that you have as much fun reading these tales as I did listening to them. May they brighten up your days, enhance your nights and fuel your own fantasies.

And if they inspire you to embark on a sexual adventure of your own that you want to confess . . . I'm *always* listening.

Happy reading,

Madame B x

HARD HAT

The only thing worse than walking past a building site and being jeered and wolf-whistled at is walking past a building site and being ignored. In a world where the rules about men and women are so blurred and unclear, it's hardly surprising that the strong, silent construction worker remains such a popular fantasy figure.

Well, the girl who told me the following tale thought that her crush on a mysterious builder was an idle daydream. But a casual fantasy grew into a sexual obsession that dominated her thoughts night and day. And then, one evening, she crossed the line from fantasy to reality. He turned out to be all she'd imagined and more — and he allowed her to be the woman she'd always dreamed of being, too.

I walked past him every day for nearly six months. At first he was just another figure on the construction site, another man working early hours in all weathers, surrounded by overweight oafs who made catcalls about the length of my skirt or the size of my tits. But there was something different about this one. Lean, not fat, he would simply watch while the others wolf-whistled. He would just stand there and look. That's all. That's all it took. His eyes would lock on to mine and although he would continue to hold my gaze rather than check out my cleavage, I could feel his eyes burn into my back taking in my whole body as I walked past. In the evening, when I walked back home, he would be long gone.

At first I only used to hope he would simply be there – my day brightened by the two or three seconds of sexy, unsmiling eye contact that he would award me each morning. I put him at around thrity-five, with a smooth, square jawline and curly, light brown hair that I sometimes saw if he was working without his hard yellow hat. I had started to slow my walk down and added a little sashay for my benefit as well as his: to buy myself another few seconds in his presence. The hot summer day I first saw him working with his top off I went out and picked up a stranger who vaguely resembled him, took him home and fucked him.

Before long, I dressed with him in mind, carefully selecting outfits that showed the curves of my figure without displaying the flesh that attracted the attention of his colleagues. The seasons changed and the weather became cooler and when I bought my winter coat, I deliberately chose one with a belt cinched at the waist betraying curvaceous breasts and hips beneath. I wore high heels to work when I'd always been a trainers-and-change-in-the-office kind of girl. His workmates noticed the change: 'Looking gorgeous today, darling,' shouted out his fat, red-faced colleague when I strolled down the street. Another articulate fellow simply yelled out the word 'Tits!' whenever I rounded the corner. But my man stayed silent, eyes that devoured and unnerved me and yet spoke a million words. I never heard his voice.

He was unknowingly in bed with me each time I had a new lover. I took home some gorgeous men that year, but I kept my eyes closed during sex: the only way to get myself off was by imagining my fantasy man on top of me, inside me, underneath me, all over me. Then, the following morning, I'd see him at work, blushing as I remembered all the things 'we' had done the night before.

As my obsession deepened, I started to question my sanity. What did I even want with this guy? Was I going nuts, believing that there was a connection between us – something behind the silent eyes? Ironically, if he were to call out something to me, the bubble would burst. As long as he stayed silent, he could be anything. And if I was honest, I wasn't sure I wanted him to cross that line from fantasy to reality. What if that body of his, so compliant and urgent in my imagination, did not live up to my dreams? And every day as I contemplated this, the office block he worked on would be a little more polished, a little nearer completion. While part of me wanted him out of my life (that's a joke – like he was ever *in* it) so that I could get on with the serious business of actually meeting someone real, part of me wanted his job to carry on for ever. I'd got used to living with this daily sexual charge that was as much a part of my morning routine as my latte. I would miss it when it was gone. I would miss *him*.

This grief – of losing something I'd never possessed – was strong enough to spur me into taking a risk. The night on which fantasy and reality collided, I left the office at my usual time, 6 p.m., and set out on my thirty-minute walk home. It had been a crisp October Friday, cold but sunny, the first of its kind that year, and the evening dusk was clear and starry. When I passed the site it looked more like a finished building than ever. There was glass at the windows and even lights in some, although the criss-crossed tape gave away that it was yet complete. The foyer was half marble slabs but the other half was a mess of exposed brickwork and trailing wires. This would clearly be an impressive interior. For the first time, I was curious about the building for its own sake, rather than just the place where *he* worked.

I stood on tiptoe and tried to peer in through a window. With a gloved hand, I rubbed away the grime to make a porthole in the glass. Through it I saw a strong, broad back bent over a workbench, a yellow hard hat and a mug of tea on the floor. I would know that back anywhere, and when he straightened up and I saw the soft tufts of his brown hair I let out a low moan. He turned around and met my eyes. Wordlessly, he broke into a smile, displaying even white teeth. It was the first time I'd seen an expression on his face other than the set, serious look he gave me in the mornings. The creases around his mouth made him look a few years older than I'd guessed, but also more beautiful, human and vulnerable with it. Then he disappeared.

Feeling foolish, I stood there on tiptoe, not sure whether to stay or go. Then the main door to the building swung open, and he was there in the doorway framed by dark glass set in marble, half-silhouetted by the soft light pouring from inside. I took in the well-developed torso inside a filthy T-shirt, tapering down via a flat belly to plaster-splattered blue jeans and a pair of sturdy, battered beige workboots. I could see where the leather had worn away to expose steel toe-caps beneath.

The serious face was back. Trembling, and without a word, I crossed the threshold, accepting his unspoken invitation. He took my hand and led me through to the dark corner of the foyer, where he had been working. It was cold inside, too, and his breath misted the air. I followed the smoky trails it made, walking in a trance. I would have followed him anywhere. A thought ran through my mind: what am I doing here? This isn't me! I'm sensible: safe. Boring, even. My instinct said, you know nothing about this man, get out now while you've still got your clothes on! But my body told me a different story, saying, you *do* know this man, you've fucked him every which way in your dreams, and if he doesn't make a move soon you're going to explode.

He let go of my hand and stood there, still silent. I was sure he'd be able to hear the pulse of my heart. Stronger still was the pulse between my legs. I was throbbing so hard down there it was painful. Slowly turning to face him, I met those blue eyes. I spoke. 'I need to know your name,' I said, my voice quivering with anticipation. I needed to hear his voice, too: you can gauge a man's body through the outline of his clothes, but you can't predict what his voice will sound like. But still he neglected to satisfy my curiosity.

'Shhhhhhhhhhhhhh,' he said, putting a finger to my lips. I moaned: I couldn't help it. His hands were warm, rough, large and strong, worn like old leather. I could taste the plaster dust on his fingers and feel the grooves and bumps of his fingerprints. His nails were short and a little dirty. I opened my lips, and he slid his finger in, probing my mouth like a tongue, his thumb rasping gently against

8

the sensitive skin on my cheek. I closed my eyes and felt another finger lightly tracing the skin of my lips. Then he suddenly withdrew his fingers, leaving me with lips parted, waiting for a kiss that didn't come. I opened my eyes.

His hands were on my waist: strong and large, they made me feel as light as anything. He lifted me effortlessly and sat me down on the powdery workbench, dirt sprinkled all over my expensive black wool coat. He gently pushed my shoulders back. I yielded to his hands and lay down, my hair, clothes, shoes covered in plaster dust and rubble but I was too turned on to care how mussed up I got. I knew then that I would let him do whatever he wanted.

I was wearing high-heeled black boots. He unzipped first one, then another, and rolled my tights down, taking my panties off with them. The warmth of my body clashed with the chill of the winter night, and heat rose from between my legs. The fiery waves pulsing through my body meant the thrill of cold air only served to wake me up and make me feel more alive than ever.

He lifted the folds of my black skirt and ran his hands along the smooth skin on my inner thighs. The combination of his rawhide hands and the softness of his touch was electrifying. With one hand on the inside of each thigh, he pushed my legs apart as far as they felt they could go. Then he pushed them a little bit further, so I felt a build up of a dull tension as the muscles tensed. I could feel his breath on my waiting pussy. I wanted him to say something, anything, but he didn't. Instead he put his lips to another use, planting a kiss directly on my clitoris. He hooked his shoulders under my knees, so that my legs remained splayed, and used his fingers to part the skin around my clit, leaving it exposed to the cold air and his warm breath. Then he went to work with his tongue, tracing tiny shapes on the skin around my clitoris, avoiding the bud itself. This was a build-up slower and sweeter than I'd ever experienced before. Round, up, down, round, up, down, teasing me and keeping it steady until I cried out. 'More.'

He understood my one-word command and slid one dry, rough thumb inside me, tracing my insides, still working my clit with his tongue.

'More,' I pleaded. 'More.'

So he slid another finger up and then another and slowly I felt that the sensation in my pussy was as intense as the one on my clit. The circling of his tongue on my clit turned to sucking and as I felt the tiny nip of his teeth on that most sensitive part of me, my body began to buck, sending clouds of dust everywhere, messing up my hair, and not caring about anything outside of this moment and what was being done to me. Then the relief I'd been waiting for came: as the pulsations in me started, he maintained his rhythm for the few seconds it took for him to be sure I was coming. And I was, harder than I ever had before, overpowering contractions radiating through every part of my body for what felt like an eternity, until he pulled his fingers away and hardened his tongue into a small, stiff peak, thrusting into my quivering pussy so that it had something to wrap around as the waves of pleasure died down. I took him by his dusty, dirty head, pulled him up to me and said 'thank you' with a long, soft kiss in which I could taste myself.

Still wearing my coat and dress, I knelt down with bare legs and feet on the uneven floor before him. I didn't take control. I didn't need to ask him to take his cock out so I could taste it. He read my mind in real life just as he had in my dreams. His jeans had a button-fly, which he undid slowly and with a trembling hand. I stayed still, lips parted, still recovering from my own orgasm but eager to give him his. He wore no underwear and, as he unfastened the last metal button, revealed a beautiful, hard dick, one excited vein running from his light brown bush to the glossy pink tip. The skin on his cock was as smooth and velvety as his hands were rough and craggy. I put my lips together to kiss the tip of it, teasing him, swirling lips and tongue around but not letting him enter me, daring him to penetrate my mouth without permission. I could feel how excited he was: a drip of clear pre-cum fluid leaked from the tip of his penis and I relished its sharp saltiness.

He let go then, and pushed himself between my lips. I let my teeth drag ever so slightly against the lower underside of him, just to remind him that I was the one in control here. For a split second, I saw his face register this tiny pain which gave way to pleasure when I ran my tongue along the length of his dick, massaging the most sensitive spot near the tip. Then he was inside me up to his balls, filling my mouth and fucking my face, deeper than I'd ever taken any man – but still not deep enough. I'd never really got off on giving head before – this is one area I've always considered better to receive than to give – but this time I wanted more of his beautiful dick deep in me, wanted to take it all the way down my throat, surrender to the gagging feeling. I moved my whole head, determined to make him let go, to cry out. He pulled at my hair, tugging it into little peaks and spikes, kneading my scalp, making me dizzy.

With a final tug on my hair, I felt his buttocks clench and knew he was at the point of no return. I gulped, wrapping my mouth round him as tightly as I could, and he threw his head back and let out a slow, low growl. I pulled back as he shot his spunk into my face, swallowing what I could and letting the rest trickle down my chin and into my cleavage. His hands were on my face again, mopping up the liquid and feeding it to me, forcing his fingers between my eager lips. Then he dropped to his own knees and pulled me to him, where we kissed until the chill of the night brought me back down to earth.

I pulled away with a shy smile and scrabbled for the clothes he'd removed in what seemed like another lifetime. I found my boots and tights crumpled in a pile of debris but couldn't locate my black panties. I turned to see my new lover holding them to his face and inhaling deeply. Then he smiled a heartbreaking smile and pocketed them with a wink.

'Will I see you again?' I asked, as his fingers stroked my face and kissed my salty lips with a tenderness that melted me. He nodded and smoothed my tangled hair.

'Are you ever going to speak to me?' I said, half-amused, half-frustrated that I still hadn't heard him speak. But he only smiled again. Confused, I gave him one final kiss goodbye and then we parted as we'd come together, his finger on my lips, silencing me.

I left him in the half-finished foyer. On the way out, I caught sight of myself in the door: mad hair, bright eyes, red flushed cheeks, covered all over in a chalky film of dust and, oh yes, a trace of semen on the corner of my mouth. I might have looked a mess, but I'd never felt more alive, or more beautiful. It was still only 7 p.m. I walked home in the cold and dark of the early evening and spent the weekend torn between the joy of re-living that night in my head and the dread of it never happening again.

He must have worked all weekend, because when I went past the building site on the Monday morning . . . it was no longer a building site at all. The tape had gone from the windows, the wires were embedded in smooth marble and the two potted bay trees either side of the entrance gave the building an air of completion and inhabitancy. The construction firm's signs had gone and in its place was a polished brass plaque discreetly stating the residence of a firm of solicitors. To say I was disappointed was an understatement. I was horrified. I was filled with panic. Where was he? How was I going to see him again? Why hadn't I *made* him tell me his name? I didn't even know the name of the firm he worked for. My mind went into freefall: I realised then that I had never really believed the adventure to have been a one-off, but the start of something else. If only I'd known he was going away so soon – I wouldn't even have showered again just to keep his smell on me. It was now clear that having experienced the reality, fantasy would never again be enough.

By the time I reached my own workplace I was resigned to bitter disappointment and barely registered that the office was in complete disarray. Polythene sheets covered half the furniture and my files were stacked in boxes on the other side of the room. I was not in the mood for this today. 'What's going on?' I snapped at Zoë, my assistant.

'Oh,' she said. 'Had you forgotten we're having the place refurbished? The builders are in for a couple of weeks as of today.' She rolled her eyes. 'So we can all look forward to sexist jokes and the smell of bacon butties for a fortnight.'

But Zoë's chatter faded into the background as a familiar figure emerged into view behind her. There he was, in his dirty T-shirt, hard hat, and, if I wasn't very much mistaken, hard-on encased in paint-splattered jeans. I felt my body turn to quicksilver with relief and lust. I was about to call out to him when he gave me a secret smile and put a rugged finger to his lips.

'Shhhhhh,' he said.

MODEL
MISBEHAVIOUR

This confession is such hot stuff that I thought twice about printing it. A beautiful, internationally famous fashion model relayed the story to me at a party in Paris. It's one that every journalist and gossip columnist in the country, the world, even, would kill for — that of eye-wateringly hip übermodel Anna Lamb and the fiery, on-off relationship with her equally famous, adrenaline-junky boyfriend, Joey. The risks they take in pursuit of the ultimate orgasm shocked even me.

I've changed her name, of course: I could tell you who she is, but I think you'll have much more fun working it out for yourself.

For twenty seconds the cobbled Milan side street was illuminated by the pops and dazzles of a hundred flashbulbs as Anna Lamb's chauffeur-driven Merc pulled up to the back entrance of a huge white marquee. Photographers risked life and limb, throwing themselves on to the bonnet of the car, pressing up against its windows. Forget the designers or the clothes: the English Rose supermodel was the real star of Milan fashion week. The car also contained Anna's boyfriend, the *enfant terrible* of the British rock scene, singer Joey Harper. A photograph of them together was such a rarity that it could sell for thousands of dollars. A photograph of them kissing could fetch up to a hundred grand. For the paparazzi, it was worth the risk.

Inside the car, Anna gave Joey a chaste peck on the cheek. Although they'd left their hotel bed only an hour ago, the urge to pull him to her and kiss him deeply and passionately already took hold. But she fought it. She didn't want to give the photographers a single shot that might make their fortunes. But more than that, she knew that if she didn't kiss Joey now, she'd want him even more desperately later.

As Anna reached for the door handle, Joey pressed a gold paper bag into her hand. 'Something to make today's show a little more interesting, baby,' he whispered. 'I want you to wear this for me,' and, when Anna raised an eyebrow at him explained, 'It's all part of the game.'

Ah, the game. They had been playing 'the game' for the six dizzying months they'd been together: drunk on lust, addicted to each other's bodies, they had become addicted to taking risks, making love almost-but-not-quite in public, daring the paparazzi to catch them at it. As Anna walked from the car to the marquee, eyes hidden from the flashbulbs behind huge Jackie O sunglasses, she thought about the adventures they'd had and felt a familiar pang between her legs. There was the time she'd gone down on Joey before a gig. On her knees, on the very edge of the stage, just out of sight of 20,000 screaming fans, she'd taken him in her mouth and made him come seconds before he strapped on his guitar. Or the magazine cover shoot Joey had interrupted: he'd walked into the studio, carried Anna to his waiting car and slid his fingers in and out of her pussy until her orgasm flushed her cheeks and ruined her make-up. Or last month, when they'd had hot, urgent sex on the hotel balcony in St Tropez: photographers so close beneath them they could smell their coffee and cigarettes. And today, Joey had a new game planned. Anna could hardly wait. She didn't know what Joey's bag contained, but she was wildly excited: the creative and dangerous flair with which Joey filled his music manifested itself in their sex life, and she always knew that whatever he had arranged, it would create – and satisfy – a breathless, desperate sexual longing.

Inside the marquee, Anna had her own dressing room. True fashion royalty, she glided through the assorted sea of clothes horses, dressers and makeup artists. The younger models, who'd idolised their icon for years, froze, awestruck: she might be nearly thirty but there was something about Anna Lamb's amazing face, coupled with that hedonistic reputation, that still stopped a room in its tracks. She kept her sunglasses on, not (as rumour had it) because she was too stuck-up to talk to the other models, or was threatened by them, but because she didn't want her glittering and glazed eyes to give away her excitement.

In the privacy of her dressing room and with unsteady hands, she tore open the bag. There was something inside, wrapped in dark-purple tissue paper. As Anna unfastened the package the paper crackled, echoing the electric excitement, almost hysteria running through her veins. The violet tissue held a pair of sheer, pale-pink lace panties, near-invisible wisps of string joined by a pale, soft pink triangle to cover her pubic hair. Not that I need it, thought Anna with a smile, remembering how Joey had shaved her pubic hair with the ice-cold blade of an antique cut-throat razor just that morning. She slipped out of her second-skin jeans and put the panties on. There was something small, cool and hard inside them, nestling directly on Anna's clitoris. She laughed out loud – at the shock of something firm and unyielding against her clit, but also in admiration of Joey's ingenuity: trust him to find a pair of knickers with built-in stimulation.

Anna could take her pick of millionaire playboys or Hollywood A-list. The fact that she fell instead for this scruffy rock urchin set the gossips on fire: journalists speculated endlessly about their enigmatic relationship. Forget column inches: Anna and Joey had column *yards* devoted to *them*. But they never hit on the truth of the matter which was, in a world full of men willing to be Anna's slave, that all she craved was to be mastered. While richer, taller, better-looking men had wined and dined her in the finest restaurants, Joey just took her back to his bedsit in the East End and fucked her. He'd kissed her roughly, then thrown her back on a dirty mattress, pinned her arms by her sides and fucked her until she succumbed to a rippling orgasm that brought her close to tears. With characteristic charm and arrogance, he bit her on the neck, slapped her arse, called her a little slut (which Anna had loved), and wrote a song for her. No other man stood a chance since.

She walked a few paces, sticking her slim hips out, noticing the way the little bump caressed her clitoris with each step. Even sat still, she was aware of it, although she had to move to feel any real stimulation. So she kept moving – crossing and uncrossing her legs, swaying her hips, dancing, letting the little nodule grind against her clit. If she wasn't careful, she'd come before she even was dressed. Anna was saved by a knock on her door.

'Miss Lamb?' a timid, Italian-accented voice approached. It was the make-up artist, ready to transform the model from beautiful blank canvas to otherworldly couture creature. Anna usually hated sitting through hair and make-up.

But this time, rocking gently in her seat, letting the frisson between her legs build and imagining how Joey would finish what the panties had started, she relaxed. She allowed herself to enjoy the stylist's fingers working on her scalp, to relish the feathery teasing of powder brushes on her cheeks, eyes and collarbones where they caressed her, the ghosts of kisses. At one point, the make-up girl had to conceal a love bite on Anna's breast – another leftover from this morning, thought Anna, reliving the way Joey had bitten down on her tit while fucking her with a delicious shiver. Anna savoured the girl's soft fingers as she applied concealer to the imperfection on the perfect body, soft pressure on a faint bruise.

Next up to attend to Anna was her dresser. The first garment for Anna to model was a sheer chiffon minidress, with a barely-there skirt. She went bra-less, and the fabric rubbed against her nipples, making them stand to attention. Anna checked herself out in the mirror, assessing not the designer's work, but whether Joey would find her attractive in it. Through the translucent, pewter-coloured fabric you could see each nipple and the contours of her breasts clearly. Good. Joey worshipped her small, round tits. This would drive him wild. And her sooty brown hair was tousled, and her eyes had the smudged-eyeliner rock-chick look he loved.

The atmosphere backstage was tense and electric: Anna

swigged from a champagne flute as her dresser helped her into a pair of vertiginous silver heels. The designer, Alessandro, was a camp, flamboyant Roman who once told Italian *Vogue* that Anna was the only woman he'd ever consider sleeping with. He came over to check that she did his creation justice.

'*Bellissima!*' he said, kissing her on both cheeks. 'You make my dress come alive, darling. Now, go and be *fabulous.*' And with that, it was time: the adrenaline rush that always accompanied a catwalk show kicked in, and Anna Lamb slipped through the white curtain and on to the runway.

The superstar model entered to rapturous applause and could feel the the heat of the dazzling lights – the runway was at least five degrees warmer than backstage. Damn! Anna hoped that her nipples wouldn't lose their erect pertness: she was very aware that Joey's eyes would be fixed on her tits in this dress, and that he would be disappointed if he didn't see two bullet-hard nipples poking through the sheer fabric. Through the white-hot glare she could just about make out the figures on the front row: they read like a *Who's Who* of the international fashion scene: magazine editors from all five continents sat knee-to-knee with movie stars. But Anna only had eyes for Joey and, executing her signature stride down the length of the runway, she scanned the sea of beautiful faces for her lover.

Suddenly she could see him there at the end of the catwalk. She took in the familiar pale skin, the mop of black hair, beautiful high cheekbones and a hint of shadow under his dark eyes (well, they'd had no time to *sleep* last night). He was holding up what looked like a small mobile phone. Anna was touched. The world's fashion press here, she thought, and he still wants to get a shot of me on his camera phone.

At the end of the runway, she was only inches away from Joey. She inhaled his familiar smell – whisky mingled with the expensive aftershave she liked him to wear. Then he held up the little device in his hand. That wasn't a mobile phone. What was he doing? She wanted to ask him what was going on but she had to stay professional: puzzled, she thrust her hips forward and gave her trade-mark pout. As she did so, Joey pressed a button on his gadget. The panties suddenly began to buzz, sending urgent waves of stimulation up Anna's clit. That the little bump in her panties was actually a tiny vibrator had not occurred to her. She was so shocked she nearly lost her composure. Her body oozed lust and her mind was reeling: he'd bought those remote-control panties they'd seen in that sex shop! Holy shit! And now he was using them to tease her before a potential audience of millions. The dirty fucker. The clever, *clever* boy.

Anna parted her lips in a pretend-orgasm face that

was only partly faked. After a few seconds, it was time for the model to stalk back up the runway, giving the audience a view of her back and giving her the opportunity to recover, her sex-flushed face could give everything away. Hugely aroused, she had trouble maintaining her carefree strut. With every step, the lace rubbed against her bare pudenda and the vibrations sent a fresh wave of desire through her body. Christ, she could do without peaking here on the catwalk – her orgasms tended to be body-rocking, head-to-toe experiences that led her to arch her back and claw her hands at the air while her legs gave way beneath her. Then, just as suddenly as they had started, the vibrations stopped. Now that they had gone, Anna wanted more. She was completely under Joey's control.

The next time she sashayed down the runway, swathed in a red silk gown, Anna thought she was prepared for the vibrations in her panties, but the sight of Joey's face made her ache for his touch. He toyed with her, flipping the current on, off, on, off until Anna didn't know when the next jolt would be. But it didn't occur to Anna to remove the panties. She had never been afraid to play his game before, and she wasn't going to back down now, on their most daring and public round yet.

The third time, in a skinny black pant suit, Anna's lust had her biting back tears of frustration: Joey turned the panties on as soon as she emerged, licking his lips as she stood before the audience, knees trembling, pussy so swollen she could barely walk and the lubrication from between her legs threatening to stain Alessandro's couture trousers. She decided that maybe Joey's little gift of lingerie would have to go after all.

The final costume was Alessandro's *pièce de la résist-ance*, a show-stopping creation that was more work of art than clothing. The shiny gown was a space-age wedding dress, a fabulous mix of sheer fabrics and highly reflective metallics. Never afraid to court controversy, Alessandro had designed the dress with a strategic slash across the bodice, meaning that the left breast was restrained by silver satin while the right one was naked and vulnerable. Anna glanced down at the exposed breast: the nipple was erect and flushed to a dark reddish-brown, telling Joey and the rest of the world just how turned on she was. She turned to look for her dresser to help her lift the folds of her gown and remove the thong, but the girl was nowhere to be seen. Frantically, she tried to tug them off herself, wobbling on her skyscraper heels.

Alessandro saw her struggling with the voluminous layers of her skirt and playfully slapped her hand away. The touch of another human being made her throb with frustration.

'You haven't got time to re-arrange yourself, darling,' he said, 'you're on!'

And with that, he thrust her out towards the cheering public.

The music changed for the grand finale. Anna almost laughed: it was the track that had taken Joey to the top of the charts, 'Beautiful Slave', the song that he had written for her after they first made love. The explicit lyrics detailing what they'd done that night: he had made her his slave then, and there was nothing she could do about it now. The buzzing started, making Anna's breath come in short gasps that were almost sobs. Her pussy was dripping and she could feel the telltale contractions letting her know an orgasm was on its way. She walked towards Joey, eyes begging him not to make her come, to let her do the day job she was so famous for, *please*! As she drew closer to him, the cameras trained on both of them – the model on the catwalk and her adoring lover – but Anna was worried they'd get another picture entirely if Joey didn't turn off the vibrator in the next few seconds.

Anna tried to exercise mind over muscle. If only she could wait until the show was over and Joey could come backstage, fuck her and put her out of her misery. But this image made things even worse, as she imagined his skinny body hovering over hers, sliding his smooth, long cock between her legs the way he had this morning. Her wetness seeped through her panties and ran down her legs threatening to stain the £40,000 showpiece dress. Her tits rose and sank as her breathing became shallow, the exposed breast visibly quivering.

This dress, this moment, was the highlight of Alessandro's latest collection. Anna had to hold her pose for ten whole seconds while lights flashed, music played and the crowd applauded the designer. She was now teetering on the edge of the runway, face to face with Joey. When she finally dared to meet his eyes, she saw him mouth the words, 'Come! Come, you little slut,' and with that, he twisted the handset in his hand and turned the vibrations up to an intensity so fast and strong that Anna was sure it would drown out the music. Short of ripping the underwear off – which was impossible – there was nothing she could do. She felt the familiar pre-orgasmic rash start to creep across her chest. Would the cameras pick it up? As she tensed her body, preparing it for the massive release of tension, she reflected that since she was going to come so hard, it was almost a shame she wouldn't have Joey's dick inside her: she'd squeeze it so tight, so tight. It was too late.

The music soared and Anna tried to strike her pose but failed. She abandoned herself to the waves that washed over her, aware that her face would be contorting and her arms and legs shaking with sheer physical pleasure. She let her eyes close because if this was professional suicide, she didn't want to see it happening. As she heard the first gasps from the audience, she was aware of a presence at her side. Joey. He leapt up on to the runway to kiss her, shielding her bucking body from the cameras and sliding his tongue subtly in and out of her mouth, muffling her cries.

'Oh, angel,' he sighed, 'You were *amazing*,' And he held her, while her pulsating body subsided. Then Joey picked her up and carried her over his shoulder back up the catwalk. The audience was silent for a few seconds. Then one clap turned into a deafening round of applause: the crowd screamed and whistled, calling their names, willing them back for more.

Backstage, Joey gently set Anna down. She slapped his face as hard as she could. 'What the *fuck* do you think you were doing?' she screamed. 'That could have been the end of my career. And you've completely upstaged Alessandro. Jesus, Joey, what were you *thinking*?'

Joey smiled. 'I think, my beautiful slave, that I was making you come harder than you ever knew you could,' he said, wrapping an arm around Anna's waist, crushing her dress. 'And I think that now I'm going to take you to your dressing room and do it again.' He steered her to her private room and closed the door behind them. Then he knelt at her feet and effortlessly lifted up her expensive dress to reveal her pink panties, now soaked with her juices. Joey put his face between Anna's legs, breathing in her musky odour. 'I can smell and taste how turned on you were up there,' he breathed. He hooked his thumbs under the sliver of lace and slid it down to her ankles in one swift movement. His hands were on her then, thumbs tracing her swollen pussy and finally her clitoris, which was still tender to the touch: far too sensitive for Anna to be able stand Joey's hands on it, making her shiver and squirm. 'Your clit might not be able to take any more,' said Joey, 'But the rest of you sure fucking can.' He got to his feet and spun Anna around so that she was looking at herself in the dressing room mirror: flushed and smudged, a fallen angel dressed in rags and tatters. Joey took Anna by her tousled dark hair and pushed her forward: bent double at the waist, she rested her arms on her dressing table and closed her eyes, desperate for a moment's peace and solitude.

But instead she heard the familiar clunk of Joey's belt buckle unfastening, and before Anna had time to open her eyes, he used one knee to part her legs and pushed himself inside her. Anna was wet enough for him, but so spent by her intense climax that she wasn't sure she could take Joey's vigorous thrusting. She opened her eyes: he was behind her, pulling her hair so that she had to face the mirror, one eyebrow raised as he rammed into her over and over again, daring her to quit now. His face, earlier so playful, was suddenly deadly serious. She saw his eyes dart all over her perfect body, and she knew he was horny just watching himself fuck her. He didn't know whether to feast on the sight of her arse or gaze on her bouncing little tits in the mirror, Anna could tell, and the most scrutinised, looked-at and photographed woman on the planet got off on it. Their mutual narcissism made her heart beat a little faster. She bent lower, to show off her arse and so that she could see more of him in the mirror: he was still wearing the battered military jacket he was famous for. Joey drove his dick into Anna so hard that her whole body jolted. Intense as it was, Anna wanted more. As if reading her mind, he placed his thumb in her mouth to lubricate it, and then deftly slid it into her arse.

With his thumb, Joey slid in and out of Anna's arse in time to his thrustings in her pussy. A shiver that began in her pelvis flowed along her limbs, numbing her arms and legs: she was oblivious to everything but the tingle deep inside her. The longer it lasted, the more she wanted it. Unable to believe she could reach another climax so soon, but powerless to resist the sensations Joey created in her body, Anna surrendered to the surge of seizures that sent pins and needles rushing through her and, writhing like an eel, she cried out this time, a long, low, wordless moan that told Joey all he needed to know.

Joey didn't let her ride out the orgasm: as her pulsing pussy hugged his erect cock, he slid his thumb out of

Anna's arse. He reached forward, desperately feeling for her tits, fingers ripping through the chiffon of her top and tearing the fabric that covered one breast, rolling nipples between expert fingers, pulling on her tits and turning her moans to screams. Anna looked like some kind of tortured mermaid, her long silver skirts like mercury on her coltish limbs, but her top half naked and vulnerable, her beautiful face contorted in ecstasy. Joey kept his hands on her nipples as he came seconds later, his head buried in her shoulder. Anna could feel every inch of his dick inside her as it quivered and jerked.

As their legs gave way and they collapsed into a pile of bones and cloth on the floor, Anna could feel her own ejaculate mixing with Joey's spunk trailing down her legs. The fabric of the skirt was sticky against her legs: the dress was ruined. She would have to pay Alessandro for it. That was cool – she could afford it, and that had definitely been a forty grand fuck.

With the tenderness that always followed their love-making, Joey peeled the fabric that was stuck to Anna's body, softly kissing his semen away from her thighs, using a wet towel to wipe the sweat from between her breasts. She returned the favour, gently pulling back his foreskin to wash under it with her tongue in a way that made him shiver.

They slipped back into the clothes they'd arrived in

and shared a glass of champagne. There was a knock on the door. 'Anna, darling?' came a familiar voice. She came back to earth with a bump. Oh shit. It was Alessandro, come to tell her she would never work for him again. His beautiful dress was a crumpled heap in the corner, covered in sweat and spunk. How was she going to explain this to him? She didn't have to. Joey opened the door, cigarette dangling from his lip and flashed Alessandro his most charming grin. 'We've got a confession to make,' he said. 'I'm afraid I couldn't wait to ravish your favourite model, so I've made rather a mess of your dress.'

'Darling!' said Alessandro, air-kissing Joey, 'You can wash the car with it for all I care. You two were *fabulosa*. You've paid for that dress a million times with all the publicity you've created for me tonight.'

'You're very generous,' said Joey, and pulled Alessandro towards him and kissed him full on the lips, lingering for just a second. The designer, clearly as delighted as he was shocked, backed out of the dressing room giggling, lost for words. Ooh, thought Anna, as she had forward-flashes of visions of the three of them entwined on expensive sheets somewhere.

❧

At the aftershow party, Anna and Joey stole the show again. Drunk on champagne and lust, they flirted with strangers and enjoyed the attention but came together to kiss whenever the photographers had their backs turned. They returned to their hotel at daybreak, a clear blue sky lighting their way through the Italian streets. Passing a news-stand, they had their driver pick up a British newspaper. A picture of their kiss dominated the front page. 'Anna and Joey: It's Love!' screamed the headline. No one had noticed Anna's public orgasm, or Joey's remote control handset.

'Well, my beautiful slave,' said Joey, sliding his hand down Anna's top and massaging the underside of her breast, 'It looks like we got away with it again. We're unstoppable, you and I. But you know what this means?' Anna was struck by a sudden panic that for Joey, now that their relationship was public, the 'game' was over. But he continued. 'This means that the bar has been raised. We now have to find ever-more beautiful and extraordinary ways to enjoy each other.' The look in Joey's eyes reassured Anna that he was already planning their next adventure. She wound down the window, breathed in the cold city air, and shivered with anticipation.

TOY STORY

Most of us have wondered what it would be like to be with a woman at some stage, although we tend to lust after distant celebrities or remote acquaintances. But the woman who told me this story found that the object of her fantasies was close to home – too close for comfort.

You know what it's like having flatmates. You start off with separate shelves in the fridge, labelling your milk, itemising the phone bill and forbidding each other from using your shampoo, but before long you're sharing everything. Clothes you swore you'd never lend anyone somehow find their way on to your flatmate when she's got a date. You know how it is.

That's how it was with me and Laura. We'd been friends since our late teens, and when we landed our first jobs in the same big city, it was a foregone conclusion that we'd share a flat together. We were as close as sisters, and had never had an argument: but perhaps more importantly than that, we just about took the same dress and shoe sizes, and definitely shared a sense of style, so by moving in together we each effectively doubled our wardrobes, and what better criteria can there be for a flatmate? Although we were the same size, we were different shapes. Laura's figure was a little fuller than mine; she was curvy where I was athletic and lean. I would never in a million years fill one of her bras. But that was cool: clothes that hung off me like I was a coat hanger came to life on Laura, her curves filling out the fabric around her tits and arse. When she wore one of my vests, she looked poured in, just about ready to burst right out of it. Whenever she borrowed my clothes, men looked at her as though they hoped the seams would split and the flesh be exposed at any moment. I know Laura got off on that. The size difference worked for me, too. I liked the way her jeans hung off my hips and left a little slouch when I wore them. Like borrowing your boyfriend's.

After a couple of months living together, we had an unspoken rule that each could borrow the other's clothes whenever she liked as long as they were back in the wardrobe, washed and pressed, within a few days. It worked so well that in a while we kind of forgot who owned what.

But things changed the day I found that I was out of clean pants. It was my turn to do the laundry, and I'd got behind with it. Borrowing jeans and dresses was one thing, but underwear . . . I wasn't sure. I padded down the hall to Laura's room to ask if she had any spares. It would be a little weird, but I thought she'd be cool. I knocked on her door. Damn! She was at the gym. I'd forgotten. Oh well: nice girls don't go commando! I'd borrow them now and have them back before she knew anything. I pushed the door open and a familiar floral smell filled my nostrils: she'd borrowed my fragrance again. On her, the light perfume took on a slightly different scent: headier and muskier. I breathed it in. I liked it.

Stepping over discarded magazines and make-up bottles, I made my way over to her chest of drawers. Knickers and bras of every kind spilled out all over. I let my fingers trail through the lace of a delicate bra, savouring the feel of the silk against my skin. I suddenly felt guilty, as though I were somewhere I shouldn't be.

Rummaging through the tangled strips of silk, cotton and lace, I saw a flash of stripy underwear in the corner and identified them as a pair of girl-boxers I'd noticed Laura lounging around the flat in. I stepped out of my pyjama bottoms so that I was naked but for my white bra. I slipped the boxers on, enjoying the way they felt. Slightly loose, so that the air could still get to my skin. I admired myself in Laura's full-length mirror. I looked good: although not as pretty as Laura.

I went to close the drawer and heard a low humming sound coming from inside. Curious, I investigated further.

My hands closed on something soft but solid. And it was vibrating. I pulled it out, and, half-wrapped in a red silk scarf, there it was: a pink, glittering vibrator, shaped like a cock. I let out an involuntary gasp. I'd seen vibrators in sex shops and reviewed in women's magazines, but I'd never had one in my hands before and I certainly didn't think that Laura possessed one. I thought we told each other everything. 'Laura,' I whispered, even though (well, because) she wasn't there to hear me, 'You *dark horse*!'

Suddenly I had a vision – and why wouldn't I – Laura using the toy on herself; running it all over her nipples, holding it against her knickers. In my mind's eye I saw her sliding it in and out of her pussy. I pictured her face in orgasm, twisted with pleasure as she came, and felt myself blushing, shame creeping in heat over my face. To my surprise though, the image turned me on. *Really* turned me on. I'd never experienced a surge of arousal like the one I felt right then, urgent, almost violent, a throb that resonated through me.

I sniffed at the sex toy, hoping it would smell of Laura, but it was clean and had a neutral, plasticky smell. It was still buzzing gently in my hand: I saw the 'on' switch which I must have triggered when I slammed the drawer shut. The vibrations travelled up my arm and towards my neck, so that I could feel them throughout my body.

Without even thinking, I held the toy against myself,

letting it murmur against Laura's boxers. Oh my God, I thought. Even through the cool fabric, I could feel how hard my clit was, standing to attention, even before it grew hot, pulsing under the vibrator's buzz. Still thinking about Laura, I pushed it closer. I could feel every fibre of the brushed cotton of her panties: soft and dry, it contrasted with the hot, wet feeling between my legs. What happened next overwhelmed me. Within seconds, my legs had started to buckle under me and I staggered to her bed. I pushed the vibe closer on my clit, feeling the moisture seep into the gusset of Laura's panties. Seconds later I had come harder and longer than ever in my life. I succumbed to six, maybe seven massive spasms of pleasure lying face-down on Laura's unmade bedclothes, breathing in her scent as the juice from my pussy soaked her panties.

Whoa! What had I just done? I stood up on shaky legs and looked at myself in the mirror again. The face I saw now was different to the one reflected just a few minutes ago: a telltale pink flush stained my neck, breasts and cheeks and my features wore an unmistakable expression of guilt. This was *Laura* – a friend who was more like a sister than anyone I'd ever known. I'd always been so straight before and here I was having my first lesbian fantasy, my first sex-toy experience and the strongest orgasm I'd ever had all in the space of a couple of minutes.

A noise in the street outside brought me to my senses

as I realised that Laura would be home any moment. I used one of her make-up wipes to clean up the vibe, wrapped it up in its silk scarf again and replaced it in its secret hiding place, hoping it didn't bear some trace of my body that would betray me. Had I wrapped it up the right way? Had I put it back in the right drawer? Laura's bedroom looked like a chaotic jumble of clothes, but she always laughed that she knew *exactly* where everything was. What would she think if she caught me? She'd be totally freaked out, that's what. I would lose the best friend I cherished and the flat I loved. I gathered my pyjama bottoms from her bedroom floor and hid in my own room. When Laura did come home, fresh from the gym and a shower, I called 'hello' but didn't go out to see her. I couldn't face her – not just yet. That night, my sleep was interrupted by uncomfortable dreams of Laura using the toy on me and letting me put it inside her. I woke twice, sweating, in the grip of a huge rush, my hands inside my pyjamas, where my fingers found proof that wet dreams aren't just for teenage boys.

The next day I shared a coffee with Laura over breakfast. She stood in the kitchen, dressed only in a light cotton wrap. She cast a silhouette against the window, I could see her breasts in profile, round and pert despite the fact she wasn't wearing a bra. Her small waist, the gentle swell of her butt and a tuft of pubic hair were also clearly visible through her wrap. Knowing there was nothing but a wispy garment between the two of us made my pulse race in a way I wasn't used to. I must have been acting a little weird, because before she disappeared into her room to dress for work, Laura looked closely at me.

'Are you okay?' she said, bending over to examine me so that I could see the dark outline of her nipples. I must have convinced her that I was fine, because she disappeared into her room and closed the door. She left me sitting at the kitchen table, nursing my coffee. Without knowing it, she'd ignited a spark of sexual arousal that I couldn't ignore.

As soon as I was sure she'd left for work, I was back in that bedroom, hands shaking as I unwrapped the vibe. This time I knew what to expect, and I'd been getting horny. I held it directly against my skin, without the panties this time. The vibe was warm, soft and slighty tacky. I fantasised that it was Laura's skin. When I closed my eyes, I pictured Laura using the dildo on me as she had in my dream. Again, I came in seconds flat, a climax that made me close my eyes and cry out, so lost in how good I felt that I didn't care who heard me.

Over the next couple of weeks I snuck into Laura's room to raid her toy-box whenever I got the chance. Occasionally, I even made myself late for work, waiting until she'd gone out so that I could pleasure myself before

I left the flat, but it'd been worth it. I'd think about the toy all day, so that by the time I got home my panties were soaking and I couldn't wait. I rushed back to be with the vibe, eager for its company in a way I'd never been with any boyfriend. My daring grew stronger. I started sliding the vibrator inside me, closing my eyes and imagining that it was Laura thrusting it deeper and deeper into my pussy. And I was spending a small fortune on batteries.

I could have bought my own vibrator, I know: I walked past a sex shop every day on my way to work. But I didn't. The fact it was Laura's toy made it twice as horny for me. It was part of her: I liked to picture her with it, and twice I'd burst into the bathroom, accidentally-on-purpose while she showered, hoping for a glimpse of her naked body to fuel my fantasies. The secrecy was an added thrill. Okay – I'll admit it. I was getting a little addicted. I'd have been happy for things to carry on like this for ever.

But two weeks rolled around and it was my turn to do the laundry again. I brought the bag of Laura's clean clothes to her room.

'Sit with me while I unpack,' she said.

Then she laid out *those* girl boxers on the bed in front of me.

'I don't remember wearing these for ages,' she said.

'Oh,' I said, gulping, my pulse racing between my legs as well as in my cheeks. Just looking at the panties took me back to the way it had felt that first time. Oh God, I was getting wet again.

'I'd been looking for them for a while. Kim, did you borrow them?'

'I might have,' I said, resorting to the feeble child's denial that always means 'Yes, guilty as charged.'

'Because we don't usually borrow each other's underwear, do we?'

I couldn't meet Laura's eye, so I shrugged.

'That means that you've been rooting around in my underwear drawer, doesn't it? Have you seen anything? Anything you want to tell me about? Anything wrapped in a red silk scarf, for example?'

She knew! I braced myself – it would be the end of my private little world – and took her silence to mean anger. I finally found the courage to look Laura in the eye.

'Oh, Kim,' she said. 'I've known about it for days. I saw a really horny film the other night and went to play with myself before I went to bed. And I saw someone had replaced the batteries. I knew it could only have been you.'

'You're going to ask me to leave, aren't you?' I said, wondering how I could have been so stupid. I turned my back on her, too ashamed to meet her gaze.

Laura didn't say anything. She's really angry I thought. she's really dragging this out. The silence was excruciating.

Then I heard the flick of a switch and a familiar buzzing sound.

'On the contrary,' she said. 'I now have an even bigger incentive to make you stay.'

I could feel the warmth of her behind me, and when she ran the vibrator down the length of my spine I let out an involuntary moan of pleasure. I sat perfectly still, although inside I was on fire. Laura trailed the sex toy over the small of my back, then rolled it between my shoulder blades before using it to press gently on the skin behind my ears. I'd once told Laura that this inch of skin was the most sensitive erogenous zone on my body and that any man who knew to kiss me there was virtually guaranteed to get me off. She exploited her secret knowledge, pressing the toy against my neck, turning the vibe down to its lowest setting where it tickled me like a feather, creating a current of arousal that flowed directly to my pussy.

Close behind me now, Laura reached her free hand around and parted my bush.

'God, you're soaking,' she said, sliding a finger into my pussy and then putting it to her lips. I felt embarrassed until she turned me around: her own legs were parted and the dew dampened her own thighs, too.

Facing each other, we kissed, the vibrator forgotten for a few seconds as we tentatively explored each other's mouths. I had never kissed a girl before, and I was shocked by how soft and warm Laura was. Kissing men, I'd always been conscious of the scratch of stubble and felt small and helpless. Now, with my lips brushing against Laura's, a woman my own size, I felt empowered, sensual, that I was about to make love to my equal. I let my hand slide down to Laura's breast, cupping it. It felt warm and heavy in my hand: instinctively, I leant down and kissed the skin above her nipple. Laura's eyes became glassy as she lost herself in the sensation. We sank down on to the crumpled duvet together, limbs tangled, lips on fire.

I lay back and Laura pulled herself up so that she was kneeling over me, her breasts dangling out of reach, her own pussy just out of sight. 'Spread your legs,' she told me, in a new, domineering voice. She placed the very end of the toy on the tip of my clitoris where she held it for a few seconds and flicked a switch, turning the toy up as strong as it would go. It was too intense: I pushed the toy away, but Laura had new ways to tease me. Kneeling over my legs, she slid the vibrator inside my soaking pussy, my fantasy girl finally enacting an image I'd played in my head, over and over again. She fucked me with that vibe, penetrating me hard, twisting it around, putting it just one-third inside me and when I begged her to fill me all the way up, she'd pull it away, leaving me empty and yearning for more.

Then she fell on me and kissed me with a passion

that matched my own. The weight of her body on mine forced our tits to rub together – her beautiful, large, soft breasts enveloping my own hard little nipples. The horniest (and most frustrating) element was that our pussies were almost-but-not-quite touching. Laura retrieved the vibrator and slid it between our hips. I dug my fingers into her back, grinding my pelvis into hers, pulling her as close to me as I could get her, the toy wedged between our two bodies, its vibrating tip stimulating both our clits simultaneously. Laura bent down for another kiss: as she took my lower lip between her teeth we came together, pulsating pussies touching, our juices mingling as we shared our orgasm. I felt that I had overdosed on sex, that I had used up all the pleasure allotted to me in the world, and that nothing would ever beat that experience. We fell asleep in each other's arms, our bodies meshed together in Laura's bed. By the time I woke up, she had already left for work.

I don't know how I got through the day. I was tempted to go and masturbate in the office loos but I wanted to save my climax for Laura. I was so horny that the bumpy tube ride home was physically uncomfortable. When I got back she was already waiting for me. I gave her a shy smile, suddenly nervous about how to make the first move. Then Laura spoke.

'I don't think it's a good idea that we share the toy any more,' she said.

What was she saying? That last night had been a mistake? I knew she'd enjoyed it too . . . did Laura have second thoughts? I had spent all day building up to fucking her again, and now there was a danger I wouldn't be allowed to touch her in the way that I'd always wanted.

'That's right,' she said, and she broke into a wide smile. 'That's why I went shopping.' And from a sleek pink carrier bag she produced a double-headed dildo, clearly built for two women.

'It's great to borrow,' she said, 'But it's even *better* to share.'

BOSSY

This woman's confession will appeal to anyone who's ever met an arrogant man who needed teaching a lesson. It took a clash with a bullying boss to bring out Donna's inner dominatrix. Her whip-cracking ways proved to be the ultimate in girl power. Some girls just do better on top.

God, he was a bastard. I watched through the smoked-glass wall as Hugh Lancing shouted at yet another member of staff. He'd been at my company for only ten days and already he had managed to piss off, upset or make an enemy of every single employee. An arrogant ex-public schoolboy, he'd called us in, one by one, to performance reviews where he'd bullied and intimidated most people to tears.

I dashed off an email to Natalie, our office manager, even though she was sitting opposite me.

'That bloke's such a wanker,' I typed.

Ping! She bounced a message right back at me.

'He's vile. But he's brilliant at his job. And if he turns

this company into a goldmine, we'll see it reflected in our bonuses at Christmas.'

I replied to Natalie: 'That's if he's got any staff left by then!'

The clock on my computer told me it was four-thirty. Nearly time to go home, but not near enough. My severe office clothes began to feel restrictive around this time of the day. In my company, dressing down was not an option. I got a buzz out of working the sexy secretary look, but after a few hours, my pencil skirt began to feel a little too tight, the crisp blouse a little too formal, and my high heeled shoes began to pinch. I longed for five-thirty to come.

Then I got an email from Lois, Hugh's dowdy PA.

'Hugh would like to see you for a progress review in his office at 6 p.m. this evening,' it stated. No 'Dear Donna', no please, no apology for the short notice. I spent the next couple of hours – resentfully – going over my recent work. If Hugh was about to pick on me and claim I wasn't good at my job, I wanted the figures to prove him wrong at my fingertips. As I scrolled through documents and spreadsheets detailing the huge deals I'd brought in over the past six months, I felt a renewed pride in my work. I might not have been born with a silver spoon in my mouth, I might not have a degree, but I'd clawed my way up in this industry using nothing but working-class savvy and a whole lot of ambition.

At five to six, I went to the ladies' bathroom with my make-up bag: a girl doesn't go into battle without the appropriate warpaint. I ran a brush through my thick, light-brown hair, and ran a slick of matt pinky-brown lipstick across my mouth. I smoothed the crisp black fabric of my skirt down and checked my top for stains. None. I looked good: successful, in control and confident.

At six sharp I was outside Hugh's office door, waiting for Lois to get back to her desk and let me in: all employees were forbidden to communicate with Hugh other than via his PA. At four minutes past six I realised that Lois had gone home for the day, so I knocked on the smooth walnut door and waited for Hugh to answer it himself. Instead, he called for me to come in.

He had a file bearing my name open on his lap and didn't look up from it as I stood in the doorway of his office.

'Donna Clarke,' he said, without making eye contact. He practically spat out my name. I remained where I was, taking this chance to scrutinise Hugh Lancing closely for the first time. He radiated power and money: from the cut of his suit – Savile Row, must be – to the understated quality of his black leather shoes. His thick hair showed no signs of thinning or receding even though he must be around forty: it fell across his eyes in a thick, dark-blond curtain. I just knew he'd had the same haircut since he was about eight. A shadow of light-brown stubble on his strong jaw was the only trace of imperfection about him. In any other circumstance, I'd have found him attractive.

Hugh chose this moment to acknowledge my presence properly and nodded at a chair opposite his desk. I sat down, crossing my legs at the ankle. I folded my arms and eyeballed him, determined not to let myself be bullied.

'On paper, your track record's not bad,' he said. 'I have you singled out for good things.'

'Thank you,' I said. I knew he liked people to call him 'sir' but I wasn't having any of that. I don't treat people with respect until they've earned it. I would just give him the bare bones of politeness but no more.

'In the future, I'd like to promote you to Department Manager,' he said, unexpectedly.

I tried not to let my surprise and excitement show. 'Excellent,' I said.

'Not so fast,' said Hugh, a sneer playing about his lips. 'You'll have to prove you're up to management material by getting rid of the dead wood first. You're going to sack five of your existing staff, first thing tomorrow. I'll see how you deal with that, and we'll take it from there.'

My blood boiled. Sacking people was his job, not mine: and if I did get a promotion, I wanted it to be on the strength of the work I could do, not on how well-developed my mean streak was. All thoughts of keeping my cool in his office vanished as anger got the better of me. I got up, took a step closer to his desk and leaned in so close I could smell mint on his breath, and he could see down my top as my breasts hung and skimmed the glass of his desk. 'You might be able to get away with this with other people,' I sneered at him, 'But I worked my way up by standing up to bigger and harder men than you, and you don't frighten *me*. You can do your own dirty work.' I sat back in my chair, and confidently waited for him to fire me. Instead of the outburst I was expecting, his features softened, and he looked eager, intrigued. The expression on his face reminded me of something, but I couldn't think what.

'No one has spoken to me like that for a very long time,' he said. I kept quiet: if he was playing a mind game with me, I wasn't joining in. 'Yes, it's been a very long time since a woman stood up to me like you just have, Donna.'

I wondered if he realised that his breath was coming in low rasps and that he was licking his lower lip: if I didn't know better I'd say he was aroused by this. Instinctively my eyes travelled down towards his crotch which I could see through the polished glass desk. Sure enough, the beginnings of an erection strained at the fine wool suiting. I raised my eyebrow at him and tutted. Hugh blushed a deep shade of pink and his bulge grew bigger, making the pinstripe stiffen.

In that second the balance of power shifted in my favour. I'd met Hugh's type before: the bully who likes nothing more than to be dominated by a woman. Here was one mind game I knew how to play – and win. I turned on my high heels and marched from his office without a backward glance, even when I heard the creak as he rose from his chair and watched me walk out.

៖

I walked the city streets, my mind racing. I'd lost my temper, sure – but I'd had an unexpected result. I'd had a couple of previous relationships where my boyfriends had wanted me to play power games: I'd been a natural, dishing out punishments and barking instructions like a true dominatrix. But these men were weak, easily led individuals. They hadn't been much of a challenge. Whereas a man like Hugh Lancing . . . the thought of belittling and humiliating this arrogant, cocky bastard made my pulse quicken and my imagination run riot. That night, I barely slept, and when I did, I had dreams about bending his body in a variety of positions, bellowing orders at him, teaching him lessons no other woman would dare to.

The next morning I paid more attention to detail in my appearance than usual. I planned to walk past Hugh Lancing's office at every available opportunity that day and had to look the business. I chose a Roland Mouret dress that skimmed my curves like a second skin: expensive, made of black crêpe, it was a dress for a woman in control. I swept my hair up into a sophisticated but severe chignon, and I swapped my contact lenses for my old horn-rimmed spectacles. Replacing my usual soft lipstick with a cruel slash of red completed the transformation. I wanted Hugh to take one look at me and know who really was in charge around here.

When Natalie saw me, she made her mouth into an O shape. 'You're dressed to impress,' she said. 'Did he give you a hard time last night?'

My resolve to make Hugh's life a living hell hardened as I recalled how he'd wanted me to sack colleagues, like Natalie, on little more than a whim.

'I can handle him,' I replied. I didn't tell Natalie about the plan that was forming in my mind and distracting me from the business of my day.

That lunchtime, I stopped outside Hugh's office to make conversation with the long-suffering Lois. I didn't look in on Hugh: that would have been too obvious. Instead, I listened to him shouting at someone on the telephone.

'Don't give me that shit!' he was snarling at the person on the other end of the line. 'You either take my offer or you lose my business.'

I inched across so that I was directly in his eyeline and glared at him angrily. Making sure Lois wasn't looking, I held my left hand out and gave it a small, sharp slap with my right. Then I pointed at him, making my message clear: he had behaved badly and punishment was coming his way. He stopped mid-sentence and stared at me, open-mouthed.

I disappeared from view but made sure I remained in earshot and heard him resume his conversation with an uncharacteristic lack of confidence. 'Oh, um, where was I?' he bumbled.

I smiled to myself. The little test I'd set had confirmed that Hugh was under my spell. Let the games begin.

That night, I decided to work late. I waited until everyone else was out of the building. It was 7.30 p.m. and the sun had well and truly set. I've always loved this time of evening – office workers spill into bars and pubs, work's over for another few hours, day gives way to night and anything could happen. The lights of the city sparkled in the background. And on the other side of that glass wall was someone I knew anticipated this evening just as much as I.

I walked into Hugh Lancing's office without knocking. In order to establish myself as the one in command, it was essential I broke as many of Hugh's rules as possible.

'What the fuck?' His abusive greeting was a reflex action, but when he saw who the visitor was, he stopped mid-sentence.

Here we go, I thought. I was ninety-nine per cent

sure I was doing the right thing, but I still had butter-flies: if I had read the signals wrong, then I'd be about to commit a major workplace fuck-up. Plus I wasn't sure my ego could take rejection from a man I despised so much. I took a deep breath.

'Donna!' he said, an eager, nervous expression wiping years from his face. 'Er, what is it?' I didn't respond, enjoying the way my silence made this successful busi-nessman squirm. Instead, I ran my hand over my dress, ironing out the formal, starchy garment so that he couldn't miss the soft curves underneath.

'I'm really very busy,' he said, unconvincingly. I took a deep breath. This was it. There was no longer room for ambiguity.

'Shut the fuck up,' I said quietly. He gawped back at me.

'What?'

'You heard me.' My voice was deliberately low so that he had to strain forward in his chair to make it out. Stalking forward, I spoke a single word in time with my every step. 'I've had enough of listening to your shit, you miserable little prick. I. Said. *Shut. The. Fuck. Up.*'

And he did. He remained silent as I walked round to the back of his chair and grabbed his tie, forcing him to sit upright. 'Let's stop pretending that you're the boss around here,' I said, my veins flooding with adrenaline.

'This is how it's going to be. You're going to do everything I say. You're going to be my slave. And you're going to fucking *love* it. Starting from now. '

Hugh sighed. The big, rich, powerful man rapidly became helpless under my command. And that cock was swelling fast again. I felt myself getting softer and wetter as he got harder and harder – always a delicious combination.

'We need to get some ground rules established,' I continued, letting go of his tie and walking around his executive office. 'You will only address me as "Mistress". If you are in even the *slightest* bit rude or insolent you will be punished. You are forbidden to speak unless I speak to you first.' He nodded, slack-jawed with anticipation. 'Get out of your chair,' I ordered him. He jumped up immediately and I made myself comfortable. The leather was still warm from where he'd sat. It felt good.

'Walk to the middle of the room,' I said, trying to keep my tone even, neutral, bored. It's not enough to control him: you have to control yourself, too; that's often the hardest challenge. I was so wired and horny I could have ripped his clothes off and fucked him on the floor then and there.

'Take your clothes off,' and when he just stood there, I started shouting. 'I said STRIP, you fucking prick,' I barked, as much contempt into my voice as I could muster.

'Faster than that!' Hugh's fingers shook as he kicked off shoes and struggled with shirt buttons. 'Don't just leave them on the floor! Fold them up!' Naked, he ran around his office, gathering expensive, discarded garments and laying them flat on a filing cabinet. When he'd finished, he stood naked before me.

I looked at his bare body. His physical frame was surprisingly muscular for someone who spent all day at his desk. He had a fine line of hair across his chest and running down to his bush, out of which protruded a magnificent, bolt-upright hard-on. It was an exquisite erection, and I ached at the thought of how it would feel inside me. But if he picked up on my thoughts, it would ruin the whole game. I would have to be patient.

I gave his dick a cursory glance. 'It doesn't impress me,' I said, curling my lip into a sneer. 'You'll have to show me what it can do.'

He began touching himself, and his dick grew even bigger if such a thing were possible. His hand was moving in steady, rhythmic strokes. I walked towards him and stood as close as possible without actually touching him. In my heels I almost came up to his height. I remained fully clothed while he was vulnerable in his nakedness. This power imbalance was the more marked the closer I got. I was so close I could count his eyelashes and identify the soft woody scent that hung about him to be an expensive, old-fashioned brand of shaving soap.

'Keep wanking,' I said, mesmerised by the movement of his hand up and down his shaft, faster and faster, hurtling towards a climax if he didn't slow down. He was in grave danger of coming before I'd given him permission – a punishable offence.

'Please, Mistress,' he begged, '*Please* let me fuck you.'

I gave his erection a tiny slap and watched the pain flash across his face.

'One: DO NOT use language like that to me,' I shouted. 'It's very disrespectful. Two,' and with this, I delivered another slap, this time to his balls, 'I did not give you permission to speak. And three,' this time the back of my hand made contact with the other side of his dick, 'Only I decide when you can and can't fuck me. And because you don't seem to understand my rules, it won't be tonight.' Although ironically, as I said this, my cunt was hotter, wetter and softer, preparing for his cock, as hungry for him as he obviously was for me.

'Keep touching yourself,' I said. Hugh's hands went to his dick again: there was a tiny red mark on one side where my ring had made contact with the tender skin of his penis. I resumed my position behind the desk and gave instructions from there. 'You're not allowed to come. You're not allowed to come until *I* say so.' He slowed down his hand movements. 'Did I say you could slow down?' I said, and spying an executive toy on his desk – those metronomic little chrome balls on strings – I set them off. 'You are to keep in time with this rhythm. I need you to be very precise. If you slow down, I will be very displeased.'

Relishing my cruelty, I sped the balls up so that they were clicking once every second. Now masturbating so quickly that his hand was almost a blur, he was clearly having trouble staving off his orgasm. I could have given the word but I didn't want to. Watching his cock darken and quiver and his face tremble was too thrilling. His blue eyes were brimming with tears and his square jaw tensed with the effort.

I knew he would come whether I let him or not. 'You pathetic little slut,' I said, and that was all it took. The horror on his face as he hit the point of no return without the permission to climax gave me a rush of power that suffused my whole body. For a few brief seconds, every single muscle in his gym-honed physique was picked out. Then his cock gave one tremendous jolt, his balls leapt up and he shot a sliver of white, pearly liquid on to the beautifully polished surface of his glass table. It missed me by centimetres.

'Another rule broken,' I said, examining my nails. 'You're really not very good at this, are you? Lick it off.'

Hugh looked incredulous and for one moment I

thought that he was going to challenge me, refuse to do what I told him.

'Lick it off!' I snarled, and, as he lapped at the liquid like a cat, 'You've let me down. I hope that tomorrow night you put in a more satisfactory performance.'

Hugh looked up from the smeared glass desktop. But I was already on my way out. I stood up from his leather chair, smoothed my clothes against the length of my body – for my benefit as much as his – and left him kneeling by the side of his desk, body glistening with sweat and the trace of his own semen still on his lips. I had not laid a finger on him or removed a stitch of clothing. I collected my bag and coat from my desk and made for the exit.

Once in the mirrored lift, I had to get myself off. I was so horny I didn't even need to use my hands: instead, I crossed my legs and rocked back and forth, using the motion of my body and the faint vibration of the lift to bring myself to a swift, efficient orgasm. As the first wave of ecstasy swept over me, my eyes unfocused: when I regained my composure eight seconds later, I was pleased to see that apart from a flush on my cheeks and slightly swollen lips, not a hair was out of place. No one would guess what I'd just been up to. The cool city air brought me to my senses, which reeled at my own daring.

❧

Staff were not allowed to email Hugh directly: all requests, no matter how trivial, needed to be sent through Lois. So at six-thirty I sent a message straight to Hugh's inbox.

'I want to see you naked when I come into your office at 7 p.m.'

His reply was immediate. 'Mistress, I don't want to displease you, but I will be on a conference call with our New York office at that time.'

My reply: 'Not my problem. Furthermore it is very foolish of you to question my authority. You will be naked at 7 p.m. this evening, and you will receive a further punishment for your insolence.'

I arrived at his office, at one minute to seven, equipped with a roll of strong packaging tape from the stationery cupboard. Hugh was naked, clothes neatly folded, no light except for one lamp and the glow of his computer. In my guise as dominatrix, I had to suppress my admiration for his firm, golden body. He held the receiver to his ear, curly cord cutting across his torso like a rope. I thought of what he'd look like tied up and utterly at my mercy; the sensation between my legs was surprisingly strong.

He was discussing share prices over the telephone. I didn't listen to the details. I walked up behind him and looked down at his lap: his dick was easily as hard as it had been yesterday. I pulled the chair out from under him, wrapping an arm around his waist at the same time, forcing his head down so that he was bent double over his desk. It was the first time we had touched. His firm stomach with its fine line of hair under my fingertips was warm and yielded to my touch.

Taking the roll of tape, I wound it around his ankles, binding him to his leather chair. Hugh carried on with his transatlantic call, his words punctuated by gasps and grunts. I wondered what his New York colleague made of this sudden change of tone. I took the long telephone cord and wrapped it around the base of his erection and balls, creating a makeshift cock-ring. I pulled it tight. Hugh's voice wavered, and he tried to wind down the phone call. 'I'm sure this is something we can wrap up tomorrow,' he said. The tinny voice on the other end of the line kept on.

I looked at Hugh's cock. Bound at the base, it grew bigger and darker with every passing second. Still he stayed on the phone. I put my finger in my mouth, using my saliva to moisten it: I then slid it up his arse, pressing forward where I knew it would give him the most pleasure. This was more than he could take: Hugh whimpered an excuse into the phone and then hung up. Spreadeagled over the paperwork that littered his desk, he let his body slacken under my touch. Quick as a flash, I pulled his wrists together behind his back, binding his hands to the arms of his chair. I pulled the cord a little tighter and slid my finger a little further up his arse. He was utterly helpless, a fact which turned both of us on more than either cared to admit.

'Keep your face down,' I said, not because I wanted to hide his face, but because I didn't want him to see the way I was rubbing the phone cord between my own legs desperate to get an orgasm out of the way so I could concentrate on the serious business of delaying his. The silk trouser suit I wore was as thin as gossamer and I'd gone without panties: the tight coils of the phone cord moving in rapid succession over my clit were as efficient as any shop-bought sex toy. If I didn't check my own lust I would lose all control of the situation. I knew that Hugh wouldn't be able to climax until I removed the cord from around the base of his cock. I unwound it in one swift movement, whipping my finger out of his arse at the same time. This double stimulation made him come violently, spilling spunk all over the papers on his desk. He was so lost in his own climax that he didn't notice the shudder that overtook my own body. I felt a drop of liquid seep out of my pussy and hoped that it didn't stain my trousers and undermine the authority I wielded over Hugh.

He collapsed back into his chair, tied up at the wrists and ankles, a helpless, pathetic man far removed from the bullying boss he was by day. His shrinking cock continued to dribble spunk all over his stomach and thighs. I longed to lick it off, but instead I walked towards him and placed a length of tape over his mouth. His eyes widened: as far as he was concerned, the game was coming to an end. But it was only just reaching its climax.

'That', I said, turning on my heel, 'is your *real* punishment; something to teach you not to treat everyone in this office like shit. You'll stay there until the morning.' And I left, without a backward glance.

The next day, we all arrived at work to find an email stating that Hugh had parted from the company with immediate effect and would not be returning. I still don't know who found him, or how he got away. It's a shame I can't take credit for his departure without revealing my secret.

I discovered from a contact that he's already in another post at an office just a few blocks away. I also hear he's back to his old bullying ways. I might swing by tonight on my way home. After all, no one gets away from me that easily. I think that man needs someone like me to show him who's really boss.

THE CAR-MA SUTRA

I'm hearing more and more confessions like this one: couples who have everything money can buy seeking new and unusual thrills together.

This exhibitionist wife gave her husband an anniversary gift neither of them will ever forget . . . nor will the couple who shared the experience with them. And hopefully, neither will you.

Steve slid the tabloid newspaper under my nose, waving it around so I couldn't fail to see the headline. It was Sunday morning and wading through the papers was part of our weekend routine, along with a pot of fresh coffee, smoked salmon and scrambled eggs and a long, lazy lie-in where we spent hours exploring and pleasuring each other.

'Another celebrity caught at it,' he said, a mischievous twinkle in his eye. 'And if I'm not mistaken, you rather fancy this one.' It was a paparazzo picture of a gorgeous premiership footballer, who'd been caught dogging – having sex in front of strangers in a car park, that is – with his pop-star girlfriend. Barely a weekend seemed to go by without some A-lister risking their reputation for the thrill of an exhibitionist fuck. Not long ago I'd casually mentioned to my husband, Steve, that I could understand the appeal of dogging and his cock leapt to immediate attention beneath his dressing gown. I dragged him straight to bed where we urgently fucked like a pair of new lovers rather than the married couple approaching their third wedding anniversary that we, in fact, are. He'd held me down on the bed, telling me how horny I'd look, legs spread on a car bonnet and imagined how it would look to a crowd, as he pounded away at my cunt.

'What of it?' I said, glancing at the newspaper and feigning indifference although my pulse had started to quicken at the mere thought of it. Lately Steve had been pushing the issue, emailing me at work with links to dogging chatrooms and taking the scenic route in the car at every opportunity pointing out places for a possible al fresco fuck. Only last week he'd researched a dogging site at a local lovers' lane, a beauty spot where, on a Saturday night, couples go along, park up and do whatever feels good in front of complete strangers. I know the area well – I drive past it every day on the way to work. It's an innocent-looking little place , but since Steve told me what happens there late at night, I'd started to have a little shiver of anticipation when I went past it. The question was, was

I ready to go there? Could I handle making our fantasies real? Talking about sex in public had re-ignited our sex life, but we'd never done anything like that before and you know what it's like when you've got a really horny fantasy on the go: you almost don't want to make it happen in case it doesn't measure up to the hot, urgent buzz of your sexual imagination.

'What of it? You know *what*,' said Steve, and although he didn't say anything more about it, he left the newspaper open at the relevant page. I read about this good-looking footballer and his girlfriend masturbating each other to orgasm watched by another couple who happened to be journalists. The female journalist described the scene in such graphic detail I knew she'd been turned on by it. I wondered if, being in a strange place in the middle of the night, a group of virtual strangers performing and watching, building up to a huge group orgasm, she, a hard-headed, objective reporter, felt as wet as I did now. Once I'd read that story, the idea was implanted firmly in my mind.

I thought about it. And frigged about it. And when I went shopping for new clothes and underwear, and had a Brazilian wax and even had the car fully washed and valeted, I kinda knew I was going to go for it. The following Saturday was our wedding anniversary. I booked a table at the Hillbank, an expensive and very romantic restaurant nearby with breathtaking views across the Peak District country-side outside Manchester, where we live. Oh, and it just happened to be half a mile from the nature reserve where strangers go to watch and be watched.

I didn't tell Steve, but he knew all the same. And I could tell as neither of us could eat much, that we were both so excited. I don't know how we managed to stay at the Hillbank until 11.30 p.m., but playing footsie under the table certainly helped get us both stoked up for the evening ahead. When he slid his foot under the table and forced my legs apart, pushing gently on my swelling pussy, the evening revved up a notch. I slipped out of my stilettos and lifted both my feet to his lap where I felt his hard-on like a red-hot poker through the the trousers of his Armani suit.

We skipped coffee and dessert and took care of the bill as soon as we could. In the car park, we shared a long, lingering kiss. Steve's hands wandered towards my breasts, but I wanted to prolong the tension, so although my nipples were aching to be caressed, I wouldn't let him touch me. I'd purposely stayed below the limit and allowed Steve a drink – as designated driver, I'd be in control of the route our journey would take. Inside the car my hands were trembling so much I could barely keep them on the wheel. Instead of driving straight home, I swung the car round to the left, heading for the notorious dogging spot.

'You horny little bitch!' Steve murmured. 'Couldn't

help yourself, could you, my darling?' We turned the lights down low as we pulled into the tiny moorland car park, sheltered by a horseshoe of trees. For a moment I thought that our low red sports car was the only one there and my disappointment was bitter. But as our eyes became accustomed to the dark, we could make out the shadow of a large, black 4x4. The tinted windows were open an inch or two, but it was impossible to know who was inside. Suddenly a little nervous, Steve and I talked ourselves up by imagining what they were like.

'The couple in the black car are young and horny,' growled Steve. 'They watch us fucking on our bonnet. His dick is rock-hard, and he wants to fuck you so badly but he can't because you're mine.'

'Her cunt is wet as she watches your dick sliding in and out of my pussy,' I said, warming to my theme. 'She sees you pinching my tits and thinks about what it would be like to put one in her mouth. I won't let her, though.' As we'd been indulging in our smutty talk, we'd been touching ourselves – a reflex action. We'd have to be careful not to come before Steve had even been inside me.

'Fuck it,' I said to my husband. 'Someone's got to make the first move.'

So he turned the ignition and flipped on the car's inside lights and sidelights so the shiny, red bonnet of our car was illuminated. Steve got out, walked in front of the car, slowly, deliberately so I could see his erection in profile, and opened my door. I followed him to the front of the car where we locked eyes for a few seconds. But we couldn't defer gratification any longer. I lay back on the warm, clammy metal hitched up the skirt of my flimsy dress and spread my legs, hooking my fingers underneath my sheer thong and flashing my pussy so that he could see how wet I was.

'Christ, you're dripping,' he said, unzipping his fly and releasing a huge erection.

'Jesus, Steve!' I said, genuinely shocked. Steve was a big boy, but I'd never seen him this big before and the sight of his super-sized cock made me even wetter. He leaned in, kissed me and started to massage my tits, already standing to attention. I wasn't wearing a bra, and he pulled down the stretchy silk of my dress exposing my breasts, light brown nipples quivering for his touch. He kneaded the flesh, rolling my nipples between thumb and fore-finger softly, the way he knew I loved. For a moment I was so lost in the connection between me and Steve, I forgot that we were not alone.

But we were jolted back to our senses when a noise came from the black car: faint at first, but then growing louder, the unmistakeable sound of an extremely aroused woman, accompanied by occasional low grunts from the man who was with her.

'Let's give them something to watch,' I said. Too impatient to take my panties off, I pulled them to one side, and Steve speared his cock into me, filling me up, overwhelming me. The lace of my panties rubbed against my clit and the base of Steve's cock, delicious friction intensifying all sensations. Sounds from the black car grew louder and more urgent. Not being able to see the other couple's faces made it even hornier. It felt more like we were giving a real performance: spotlit while they watched from the dark, like an exclusive private cinema showing a one-night-only live sex show. I arched my back, pushing out my tits so they caught the light. Steve's trousers were around his hips, exposing the small of his back, but he was otherwise fully clothed. I paused to unbutton and lift his crisp white shirt over his head. I wanted to feel the soft fuzz of his chest rub against my own skin, and I also wanted the woman in the car to have an eyeful of my beautiful, sexy husband. With my stilettoes, I eased his trousers down around his ankles, his tanned arse like two pale-gold globes in the half-light. My silk dress lay, belt-like, in a puddle around my waist and the harder Steve moved inside me, the more my panties rubbed at my clit. I needn't have worried that I wouldn't be wet enough to take Steve's huge dick: as he fucked me I felt a trickle of excess juice ooze out from my cunt and run down the middle of the car bonnet. Steve pulled out of me with a speed that made me gasp and bent down to the bonnet, licking it clean with his long, firm, pink tongue.

The rhythmic breathing from the other car was getting louder and it rocked gently on its wheels: a sexual sound-track of his deep baritone groans against her soft sighs. I pictured them sitting in the front seat, masturbating each other, her hand on his cock like a gearstick, his fingers working away between her thighs. I couldn't be this horny without a dick inside me, so I spread my legs and Steve was on me and in me in seconds, his hot, smooth dick bigger even than it had been a minute before, stretching my pussy. He slid one expert hand between us and circled my clit with gentle but rapid movements, sending waves of desire pulsing through my body and triggering that series of responses that builds up before a body-rocking orgasm. I felt my legs become weak and my thighs start to tremble. The harder Steve thrust, the more the base of my spine scraped against the metal of the car. Concentrating on this tiny pain was the only thing that stopped me from coming right there and then and I wanted to delay the exquisite pleasure for as long as possible. My face contorted and I made my hands into fists, fighting the urge to let go and surrender to orgasm.

'Oh no,' said Steve, recognising the signs, 'not yet. We're making this last as long as we can,' and, with a swift movement, he pulled out of me, making me gasp as the tip of his penis traced the quivering lips of my pussy on exit, and flipping me over like a ragdoll so that I faced the windscreen and my tits and belly pressed against the bonnet. He spread my legs and was inside me again with an ever-growing hard-on that threatened to split my body in two.

We stopped mid-thrust when we heard the soft click of a car door and knew that the other couple had finally left their vehicle. They were so close that I could smell their mingled scents: her designer perfume, his expensive after-shave, and underneath that, floating through the twilight, something else, the unmistakeable musk of a man and a woman ready for each other, the infectious aroma of pre-sex. Because of my position, and the pools of light and shade that the headlamps cast in that little glade, I couldn't make out their faces, but I could see their bodies – and what bodies they were. Hers was tiny, tanned, fashion-model perfect: like me, she was wearing only a slip of a dress, a slinky sequined wisp which she pulled up and over her face so that only her long, honey-blonde hair was visible. Her smooth caramel skin was the same colour all over, and her pubic hair was waxed into a neat dark-blonde strip. As we caught a glimpse of her cherry-coloured cunt, Steve resumed his thrusting, taking things slowly this time so we would be able to focus on what we were about to see, as well as our own screwing. The man was naked: his physique perfect, like an ancient Greek statue, but carved in mahogany rather than marble. He was perfectly proportioned : a masterpiece of rippling muscle inside dark, nut-brown skin. He was hairless but for a patch of tight black curls above his magnificent, arrogant cock. He was circumcised and his penis stood to attention above a pair of smooth brown balls that weighed heavy with spunk and expectation. For perhaps a minute, his body was turned towards us, watching as my husband fucked me slowly from behind. Then he turned his attention to his lover, who waited patiently for his dick, spread out against the bullbars of their 4x4 like a tiny golden starfish. I saw him lift her up and sit her on the bonnet, where he slid his cock into her. She wrapped her legs around his waist and they began rocking against each other, vocalising their pleasure, their moans growing louder with each swaying movement.

Steve and I slowed things down again to give the other couple time to catch up, breathing deeply and evenly for as long as we could. From the corner of my eye, I saw that her back too was scraped against the metal of the car. The knowledge of the tiny pain she'd be experiencing was an electric turn on for me and I could imagine the delicious fuck she was getting as well as enjoy my own. Steve must have thought so too.

'God, I'm gonna lose control,' he whispered into my ear, and he thrust hard, so hard that our car rocked as he put his whole weight behind me. Deftly he slid one hand on to my hip and made a series of tiny frantic tugs on my panties that were almost more than my engorged and tender clitoris could take. Face down on my car, I flung my arms wide, half my body falling over the edge of the car, preparing to let go and surrender to my orgasm. 'Not yet, darling,' Steve whispered, although he didn't let up the pressure on my clit to tease and test me.

And then the woman next to me reached out her perfectly manicured hand and let her fingers touch mine. That tiny touch – the only time we two couples came into contact – was all it took to propel me headlong into an overpowering climax, the like of which I had never experienced before. She kept her hand on mine as she had her own orgasm, letting out a tiny cry, like birdsong, as her partner buried his face in her breasts and shot his spunk into her, mumbling, 'Oh, fuck, oh, fuck,' over and over again in a deep voice.

Seconds after I succumbed to my climax, Steve came too, his jagged thrusts letting me know that this also was an unusually intense orgasm for him. Spent and exhausted, we leant against the car for a minute or two, letting our mingled juices travel down our thighs and over the car. Steve stroked my hair and told me he loved me. Lost in each other, we again almost forgot our companions until they pulled apart. When he pulled out of her, his cock was glossy with spunk. As she bent down and put her lips on his subsiding erection, licking it clean, I saw her face for the first time. Her features were partly obscured by a messy curtain of blonde hair, but there was no mistaking her – the chart-topping singer who was engaged to a certain notorious premiership footballer. Sure enough, when my gaze travelled upwards I found myself looking at the face which had appeared on the front page of my Sunday tabloid just days ago. As she gathered her dress and he strolled round to the driver's door, he winked in our direction and she gave us a shy, satisfied smile. Seconds later, they had vanished behind their blacked-out windows once again. Steve and I looked at each other in disbelief as their engine purred and the couple drove off into the night.

'It couldn't be *them*,' Steve said. 'Could it?' All the way home, we couldn't help bursting into stunned laughter, high on our own experience and the shocking knowledge of who we'd shared it with.

The following Sunday, the papers printed a picture of the same two celebs at a film premiere. She wore a low-cut backless dress, and at the base of her spine was a small scar – as though she'd grazed her skin while someone took her roughly against the painted metal of a car bonnet. And then I knew I hadn't imagined the whole thing. I shivered at the memory of the sexy secret I shared only with my husband and the most famous couple in the country.

STEAMING

❧

You'll never think about massage parlours the same way again after reading this sizzling little tale. I vividly remember the girl who told me this story: some women just blossom and bloom after a satisfying sexual encounter, and she was still glowing with pleasure weeks after the event.

You know that feeling when you're so stressed out that the symptoms are physical? When your shoulders stiffen and ache as though they've been set in concrete, and the furrow in your brow is in danger of becoming a permanent fixture? Not a good look. That was me last November. I'd been working late into the night Monday to Friday, and weekends were spent hunched over my laptop catching up on work I hadn't been able to squeeze into a seventy hour week. I felt more like a automaton made of metal and on overdrive, than a female of flesh and blood – and about to go into meltdown. My sustenance was coffee, cigarettes, corporate lunches in faceless restaurants during the day and microwave meals for one in the evenings. Exercise was out of the question. As for sex – yeah, *right*. I couldn't remember the last time I'd even been touched. You forget what a man's hands on your skin feels like after the first six months, and beyond that you just begin to shrivel up. If anyone had tried to touch me they'd have found me brittle and impenetrable. But no one did. I'd been meaning to book myself a pampering massage, to take time out, relax and unwind. But there was always something else, something more important, that had to be done, and I'd never got round to it.

After a particularly gruelling day of meetings, I left the office at 7 p.m. – early for me in those days. I stepped into the lamplit darkness of early evening to find that it was raining. Unable to face the wet walk to the Tube, less still a crowded and steaming commute, I decided to hail a taxi. Cabs are always scarce when in grim weather and spying one on the opposite side of the road, I made a dash for it. I opened the right-hand door just as another woman climbed in the left. We glared at each other for a second, neither of us willing to relinquish the taxi. The cabbie came to our rescue.

'If you're both going the same way, why don't you share?'

The woman's destination was only one street away from my own, so we decided to share and settled into a companionable silence. I looked at the other woman. She was like me: late twenties, dressed in the corporate uniform of slinky black trouser-suit and sharp shoes, with the same blow-dry and highlights that every other young female professional in London has adopted. But, unlike me, her face was a picture of serenity, and she smelled exotic – of musky spices, cinnamon, ginger, as if she was freshly baked from the oven. And I was aware of how rigid I was next to her: she stretched out like a cat, her movements fluid and her body limber within her tailored clothes. Grumpily, I attempted to flex my own body and release some tension: knuckles cracked and my knees creaked as I did so.

'Ooh,' said the woman. 'That doesn't sound good.' I began to tell her how sore my neck and shoulders were and how I'd give anything to get rid of it.

'What you need is a good massage,' she said, smiling and for one awkward minute I thought she was about to offer me one. I mean, I'm as tolerant as the next girl but an impromptu massage from a strange female in the back of a London cab? Hey, I wasn't that stiff and knotted up that I'd have a lesbian rub-down from a stranger. 'I used to feel like you,' she continued. 'But I know this amazing specialist spa. A sort of a Turkish, hammam type place. It's a steam bath – you come out and you feel like you've just melted. Bliss. In fact, I've just come from there.'

I racked my brains: the block where my office was boasted a few sandwich bars, a couple of hairdressers and one very exclusive gym but I certainly couldn't think of any Turkish baths in my district.

The woman leaned in close and her voice dropped to a whisper. 'They don't take just *anyone*, I'm afraid,' she said, confidentially. 'They only take recommendations from current clients. You can't just walk in off the street.'

'Oh please,' I begged her. 'You said yourself I needed a massage.'

'But can I trust you to be discreet?'

I couldn't be bothered to play these games. 'It's only a bloody massage parlour,' I snapped. 'Do you know what, I'll find it myself.'

'Sorry,' she said. 'I just need to check you're the kind of person they want. You're feisty and you seem pretty open-minded.' She smiled. 'I mean, you have to take all your clothes off in there. Would you have a problem with that?'

'Honey,' I told her, 'I've had a Brazilian wax before now. If I can sit through that with a straight face, a little steam-bath nudity is the least of my worries.' That broke the ice, and she pulled out a little red leather-bound diary from her bag, scribbled something down on a page, tore it out and handed it to me. 'That's Adi's number,' she said. 'Tell him Cassie sent you.' She thought for a minute and then added, 'If he offers you anything extra, do say yes, and – oh!' Cassie interrupted herself and I wondered what she had been going to say. 'This is me.' She handed me enough money to cover her share of the fare and leapt into the rainy street and was gone. I looked at the mobile number in my hand.

Once inside, I ran a long, hot bath and poured myself a glass of wine. The combination of the alcohol and the hot, hot bath went some way to relaxing my rigid shoulders. This only served to make me realise how tense I'd been. I decided to call the number Cassie had given me.

'Hello?' the voice that answered was smooth, with a trace of a foreign accent I couldn't quite place.

'Is that Adi?' I said, suddenly shy. 'Um, my name's Helen. I'm a friend of Cassie's, she recommended your services to me. I wonder if I could make an appointment with you. Tomorrow? Great.' I jotted down the address he gave me. It was in the same area as my workplace yet it was a street I'd never heard of.

The next lunchtime, I made my way down a small, cobbled lane I'd never noticed before. When I reached the address there was only a dull and unpromising metal security door. Wondering if this really was the place, I rang the bell, informing them I had an appointment with Adi. A buzzer sounded, the latch released and I stepped out of the grimy London day into another world.

The vast space was dominated by a gilded marble staircase. Mosaic fountains played, petals floating in their pools.

The scent of exotic spices and oils floated on the air – I lifted my nose and inhaled the warm, comforting aroma of saffron, cinnamon and rose oil. Behind a huge marble desk sat the most beautiful young man I'd ever seen: he was dressed in simple white robes which flattered his warm olive complexion. Soft black curls framed a youthful face and when he saw my awe-struck face, he broke into a wide grin, pink lips parting to reveal even, white teeth.

'Helen?' he extended a smooth and perfectly mani-cured hand out to me. 'We've been expecting you. It's your first time, isn't it? Let me tell you how we do things here. We take payment first if that's okay with you.' I hadn't asked about money on the phone, but meekly handed over my credit card. I was taken aback when he charged me £200 for a treatment yet to come, but I let it go. I was a savvy businesswoman, used to complaining when things didn't go my way. If it wasn't worth it I could always get my money back later. And I believe you have to pay a premium for top-quality service. I just kept thinking of how serene Cassie had looked. If, an hour later, I emerged with half her radiance, it would be money well spent.

The young man took me through a huge pair of gold, leather-studded doors to a changing area panelled with dark wood. 'Inside your cubicle, change into your robe,' he said. 'There's a locker key for your bag and clothes. Take a shower and then when you're ready, make your way into the steam room. Have you ever had a hammam treatment before?' he asked, and when I shook my head, he smiled that devastating smile again. 'Oh, your first time is *always* the best. You'll be scrubbed to within an inch of your life, but afterwards you come out feeling as soft as a kitten. Even I have it done,' and he extended an arm for me to feel. Underneath the curly dark hairs, the skin on his forearm was soft as a baby. I pictured the down all over his body, whether there was any on his chest, what it was like lower down, but snapped myself out of that reverie before it got out of control.

The man left me on my own. I took a shower. The gold showerhead directly above trickled soothing water infused with essence of bergamot and sandalwood all over me. There was a rich body wash in a dispenser beside me, and I massaged it into my skin, working the milk and honey ingredients into a lather over my breasts. I soaped between each of my toes, under my arms and between my legs, closing my eyes and pretending that my hand was that of the young man who'd just shown me around the spa. Relishing the fantasy, I let the water wash me clean. Finally I turned the shower off and stood naked for a few seconds, letting the last few remaining bubbles on my breasts and arse dissolve.

I felt better already. Wrapping the white towel around me, I pushed through a door marked 'steam'. I found myself in a dense haze. After a minute, my eyes adjusted to the white cloud and I could make out the contours of a marble steam room, huge, high-ceilinged and filled with women. Mostly naked women. Many had abandoned their towels and lay on marble slabs, eyes closed, blissfully relaxed. One or two of them even splayed their legs. The combination of the heat and the sweat and the light smell of all these bodies made my heartbeat quicken. I felt that familiar twinge between my legs that I hadn't felt for months, and I thought that it was such a shame there were no men here to take advantage of me. Ah, well. I was already more relaxed than I had been for a long, long time. De-stress first, and I could think about sex later. I spread my towel on a hot marble bench and lay down, feeling the vapour turn to condensation on my skin, beads of sweat and steam rolling between my breasts.

'I could just stay here all day, couldn't you?' a girl next to me asked in a lazy, sleepy voice.

'I've only just got here, but I like it so far,' I replied. 'I haven't been here before.'

'Ooh . . .' she breathed, her voice slow and unhurried. 'Who are you seeing?'

'Adi,' I replied.

There was a collective intake of breath and then a sigh, like a wave of tiny orgasms rippling over the women surrounding me. Someone stifled a giggle.

Oh!' said a voice in the mist. 'Lucky you!' More giggles and sighs came, but before I had time to ask what they meant, a male voice called my name through the mist.

I gathered my towel about me and went through a pointed arch, down a tiled corridor and into a smaller chamber where Adi was waiting for me. He was astonishingly good-looking: tall, broad and well-muscled, he wore a white robe that showed off tight buttocks and strong arms and legs. He smiled and gestured towards the stone slab in the middle of the room.

'Please,' said the voice I'd recognised on the phone. 'Helen. Make yourself comfortable.' And with that, he took away my towel so that I was naked in front of him. Feeling clumsy and vulnerable, I lay face down on the slab and closed my eyes. The slab was hot and felt good against my skin – the same warm, baked glow you feel on a beach holiday when you've spent the day lying out in the sun.

Without further warning, Adi began to work on my body, taking a loofah and scrubbing my skin hard and fast. He left no inch unexfoliated, working his way up from my feet. He used the loofah to make small, harsh circles on my skin, so intense that they burned. When he worked on my inner thighs I had to stuff my fist in my mouth to stop myself from crying out in pain. He made sweeping motions along my buttocks, pummelling and scrubbing deep into my flesh, scraping up and down my back, bringing the surface of my flesh to life wherever he touched it.

As he polished my skin, I could feel something inside me melt, give way, dissolve. The body that had been tense and rigid for so long was finally coming back to life. Adi bent double to scrub my back. His breath on my skin unleashed months of pent-up sexual frustration and I felt sensual, alive to the touch, turned on. Wildly turned on. The front of my body ground into hot stone slab: I could feel my nipples hardening and, between my legs I could feel a pulsing heat start to spread. I wondered how much Adi could see in the half-light and the steam. Part of me wanted him to know about this unexpected wave of horniness that had engulfed me since I'd arrived. As the pulse in my pussy turned to a throb, I knew I was getting wet. I hoped that the soapy water splashing between my legs wouldn't wash away my own cunt juices and that the sweet spicy scent wouldn't overwhelm my own natural aroma.

'Please turn over, Madam,' said Adi, turning his back while I slithered all over the marble, propping myself up on my elbows and eventually made myself comfortable on my back. If Adi hadn't guessed that I was turned on before, he would now: my face was flushed, my nipples were stiff and my clitoris was so engorged I was sure it would be visible. If he noticed, he was too professional, or polite, to say anything, and began his routine of scrubbing and polishing again, working his way up the front of my legs. His hands crept further and further towards my pussy, working on my knees, then my inner thighs, so close that I thought he was about to touch my clit – and I wouldn't have stopped him. But with his fingers just inches away from my bush, he switched his attention to my arms, then my stomach, swirling, soaping and scrubbing, avoiding my breasts even though they were silently pleading for his touch.

'A colleague will join me for the next stage of your massage,' said Adi, hands pummelling my lower abdomen. 'For the four-handed massage. It's our signature treatment here.'

I nodded, even though I wasn't sure I could handle any more stimulation: if one pair of hands got me this worked up, wouldn't four tip me over the edge? Then again, maybe his colleague would be an unattractive old man much less likely to increase this, frankly, randiness, whose presence would calm me down so that I could enjoy this for its own sake.

A door clicked, and in walked the guy from the reception. The one I believed to be the most beautiful man I had ever seen in my life. Oh dear.

'This is my colleague, TJ,' announced Adi.

'Hello again Madam,' he said, smiling the perfect smile that had kick-started my arousal when I'd first arrived. 'I hope you're enjoying your experience so far.'

Adi grasped my arms and TJ took my ankles: the two men stretched me in opposite directions like I was on a rack, so that my whole body lengthened and loosened under their grip. My naked torso was exposed, beads of sweat rolling between my tits, along my hips, between my legs. Each tiny bead of sweat mingled with remnants of salty water and the sensual oils I was covered in, tickling me all over. This wasn't a massage, this was multi-sensory foreplay!

TJ kneaded my feet while Adi massaged my arms and wrists. Male hands on these much-neglected areas was achingly intimate. As their expert fingers melted away the tension, I was aware of how much stress I'd been carrying around in the hands that clawed over a keyboard all day, and the feet that dashed from meeting to meeting in unforgiving high-heeled shoes.

Then they worked their way up, TJ touching the insides of my ankles, Adi caressing the soft, sensitive and neglected skin on my neck and shoulders. I couldn't help it: instinctively I let out a whimper and parted my legs. If they wanted me to beg for it, I was on the verge of doing so.

And then they were there – Adi's soft, strong hands drawing circles around the flesh of my breasts, almost-but-not-quite touching my nipples which stood up like bright red buds. TJ, meanwhile, was deftly massaging my inner thighs, my pussy juices mingling with heady perfumed oils. I looked at them. They moved in perfect time together, their hands caressed me with more skill and sensitivity than any lover ever had, but their deadpan faces betrayed no signs of arousal: I was desperate to break through this dedication to their craft and persuade them to fuck me.

In the end, I can't say I mustered up the courage to ask for more: it was more an involuntary request, issued from my lips before I knew what I was saying. 'Please,' I said, 'I want you inside me.' I didn't care what they thought: I didn't care which one of them serviced me: I didn't care about anything but the aching void in my pussy that needed to be filled before I lost my mind.

'Ah,' said TJ. 'I think Madam needs our gold-standard treatment. Two dicks reach the parts that hands fail to satisfy.' I couldn't believe what I was hearing: sure, that's was what I'd wanted! Then it dawned on me – why Cassie had told me that I'd need to keep an open mind here. These guys weren't regular masseurs, they were gigolos! I'd been right in thinking that the service so far had just been foreplay – they'd obviously been waiting for me to allow them to take the massage to the next stage. Suddenly the £200 price tag seemed like a bargain. I got to my knees and watched Adi and TJ take off their white uniforms. Each had a smooth, almost hairless body, their brown skin shining in the steamy atmosphere. As they used their hands to bring their dicks to life, their movements remained smooth, synchronised.

Adi lay back on the slab and I crawled over him on my hands and knees. I let him use the tip of his penis to stimulate my clit, tracing patterns on my cunt lips with the same steady rhythm that made him such a good masseur. I couldn't stand any more teasing and, using my pussy to locate the tip of his hard-on, I pushed down with all my weight, sighing as his dick finally filled me up. He pushed upwards as I bore down on his erection so that our hips were grinding together. But it still wasn't enough: the expert foreplay I'd been indulged in had made me greedy. I wanted more.

TJ stroked up and down my spine with his oily hands, his fists making circles that kneaded the small of my back. His voice drifted through the vapour, 'You have a beautiful, beautiful arse, Helen,' and as he poured warm oil between my cheeks, I let out an involuntary sigh, realising what was coming next. He slid a smooth finger inside my arse and circled it around, loosening me up. I'd never been penetrated in the arse and pussy at the same time, but I knew it was the only way to satisfy my craving for the ultimate completion. Rubbing my clit harder than ever against the base of Adi's dick, I raised my derrière a little, giving TJ a better view. He took my hips in his hands, and in a split second he was inside me, spearing his way into virgin territory. I held two men inside me, snug and tight: it was the most intense sensation I'd ever felt in my life. Finally, the tension I'd been holding in for the last six months melted away. Adi was still thrusting powerfully into my pussy while TJ probed my arse more gently. I was acutely aware of each dick inside me, competing for my attention. I felt my climax welling up and could tell from the increasingly frantic rhythm of Adi and TJ's movements that they were close, too.

Adi reached his hand up to my breasts and held gently on to one nipple, twisting it gently. That tiny sensation, a sharp contrast to the huge feeling in my pelvis, was all it took to bring me to orgasm. I let go and let wave after wave of spasms come across me. I felt my cunt flutter like an eyelash around Adi's cock: the secondary contractions made it tighten around TJ: both boys shot their spunk into me, finally losing their professional cool as they abandoned themselves to their orgasms. When we were done, I squeezed my whole pelvic floor tightly, letting them know that although it was over, I wanted to keep those cocks inside me for as long as possible. When they eventually withdrew from my body, my whole being felt fluid, alive, released. TJ and Adi discreetly backed out of the room, leaving me face-down on that stone slab in a pool of oil, water, soap and come. As they left, TJ gestured towards another door, twice as tall as I was.

I pushed my way through and found myself back in the relaxation area: it was now empty save for another woman, reclining in her towel. Her confident posture and expression told me it wasn't her first time here. After taking five minutes to compose myself, I returned to the changing area where I showered, taking care not to wash away the oils from my skin. I dried myself and got back into my clothes. My skin, which had been dull and unresponsive for so long, was finally alert to every different sensation: even my clothes seemed to caress me, the silk of my blouse against my skin, the lace thong that parted my arse cheeks and stroked my clit, reminding me of the pleasure administered in the hammam. I tidied myself up in the mirror. My complexion had a healthy, youthful glow and my hair had fallen into soft waves in the steam. I left through a side door. My body was made of milk and honey and the cold, grey London afternoon couldn't bring me down. I looked at my watch: I couldn't believe it had only been ninety minutes.

On my way back to work, I passed a young woman in the doorway of an austere office building. Expensively dressed, she was juggling a mobile phone with a cappuccino and a copy of the *Financial Times*. The crumpled, stressed-out expression on her face mirrored that of my own less than twenty-four hours ago. I waited for her to finish her phone call. I had another number to give to her.

A WORKING GIRL

There's a lot of things nice girls aren't supposed to do. Being paid for sex is one of them, but you'd be surprised how many women I speak to that have tried on the world's oldest profession for at least a night or two. This is by far the most orgasmic account of one woman's experience of prostitution I've ever been told.

It takes a lot of money to look like me: the red-gold highlights that I never allow to grow out, the always-matching underwear, the bikini line that's freshly waxed, the must-have bag, skyscraping heels in this season's colour plus cabs everywhere because I can't walk in them. You name it, I've gotta have it: from my personal trainer to my weekly massage, I'm a regular Park Avenue Princess.

Shame, then, that I'm a magazine assistant struggling on a salary that barely covers the basics of food and shelter here in Manhattan. The difference between my champagne lifestyle and lemonade budget came to a head last year, when I finally sat down and looked at my finances, confronted the credit cards I'd used to pay off the store cards, the overdraft that grew every week, and the loan I couldn't pay back. I was out of my depth to the tune of about $50,000. And I had no way to raise that kind of cash.

I couldn't tell anyone at work about my predicament. At the upscale magazine where I work, we have a weird attitude to money: we don't talk about it. Probably because it's never been an issue for most of my co-workers. The staff consists almost exclusively of pampered white girls who've had money since the day they were born: their Upper East Side apartments have been in their families for generations, and if they run out of cash, they can call Daddy and he'll have his accountant wire a few hundred dollars to keep them going till the end of the month.

But when you're losing sleep over your debts, something's going to give, and one day Annabel, my senior assistant, found me crying in the toilets. She's the last person I wanted to witness me in tears: blonde, sleek, upper-class, she's the embodiment of perfect poise. For her to see me lose it like this meant I could kiss my chance of promotion at the magazine goodbye.

'Kerry!' she gasped when she saw me, mascara running down my face. 'What's happened?' I blurted it all out – the mountain of debt, the pressure I'd been under to maintain a perfect glossy exterior. I knew that letting my guard down like this would result in my becoming a social outcast, but what the fuck? At this rate I'd have to leave Manhattan within a couple of weeks anyway. And it felt so good to finally confess to someone about my double life: the relief was immense, like taking off a layer of clothing on a sweltering day. To her credit, Annabel didn't judge me or tell me off: she didn't say anything, just let me talk, and fetched me a Kleenex to wipe away the tears.

'Poor Kerry,' said Annabel when I'd finished. 'It doesn't have to be like that. There's always something you can do.'

'Yeah *right*,' I said, looking at Annabel's Diane Von Furstenburg dress, this season, hundreds of dollars' worth of stretch jersey cotton that showed off a flat stomach and pert bottom – she'd been whipped into shape by the same personal trainer I used. 'This salary's just pocket money to you – for those of us without rich parents to back us up, it's all we've got. I can't just pick up the phone and ask for a handout.' As soon as I'd made the dig, I felt bad. Annabel was a lovely girl: it wasn't her fault she came from money. And I was sure she hadn't meant to be insensitive.

'Sorry,' I said. 'That wasn't fair of me.'

'No,' said Annabel, and she looked deep in thought. 'No, I can see why you'd think that. I felt the same way when I was in your position. But the truth is, most of the girls on this magazine make their own money: me included.'

'Don't be ridiculous,' I said. 'No one can live the kind of life that we do on this salary.'

'You can take on extra work on the side,' said Annabel.

'When? I'm here 8 a.m. til 8 p.m. every day. I only have about four free waking hours every day. The only extra work I could take on would be as a goddamn escort!'

But Annabel didn't laugh at my joke. She looked me in the eye and nodded, slowly. It took a minute or two for the realisation that she wasn't joking to dawn.

'Christ, Annie!' I said, mouth falling open as I realised that my cool, classy co-worker was the features assistant by day and a whore by night.

'You and who else?' I managed.

'Most of the junior staff,' she said, matter-of-factly. 'Just for a couple of years, until we can live off our regular salaries. Just a few nights a week and you can have your debt cleared in say, six months.'

'I had no idea!' I said.

'You can see why it's not something I advertise,' she said, curtly. 'And I'm telling you this on the condition that you keep it to yourself, just like I won't tell anyone what you've just told me. But I might be able to help you out. Stand up.'

I did as she said, feeling ridiculous as Annabel circled me, inspecting my figure. Under the harsh strip lighting of the office toilet I felt naked under her gaze.

'Good tits,' she said, 'And your colouring means you're unusual – you can get more money for that.' I felt my pale skin blush red as Annabel held a tendril of auburn hair between her thumb and forefinger.

'Okay,' she decided. 'You're very different looking to me: I wouldn't recommend you if I thought we'd be in direct competition. I think Mark can get you work. He's my, ah . . . we work for Mark. He finds clients for us. Anyway. Just go see him: he's a nice guy, not a monster. He'll talk you through the way it works, how much you can charge. If you don't like it or you get freaked out, just make your excuses and leave. There's no pressure.' And she handed me a business card with the words 'Mark Lenster,' embossed in silver letters on a stiff cream background, and a fashionable TriBeCa address.

For the rest of the day, I kept the card in my pocket, my fingers tracing the raised letters on the business card, reading the words like Braille. What if? I wondered. What if? I was certainly highly skilled in the bedroom, although I'd never thought about it in money-making terms before. My pale pink pout had been wrapped around dozens of grateful cocks: every man I'd ever gone down on told me it was the best oral he'd ever had. One guy even cried with pleasure, saying he'd never known a woman's mouth could make him come that hard. But I gave head because I loved it: doing it to some stranger in return for a stack of dirty dollar bills was a different story. I went back into my dark little flat, stuffed with clothes and shoes I'd bought with borrowed money. My heel spiked a bailiff's letter that had landed on my doormat. Suddenly it seemed as if I had little choice.

I made myself a strong vodkatini, curled up in my only chair and punched Mark Lenster's number into my cellphone. The voice that answered was clipped, old-money, educated New York, but he was warm and welcoming rather than intimidating.

'Hello Mark,' I said, emboldened by the drink. 'My name's Kerry. I'm a friend of Annabel's.'

'Hello Kerry,' purred Mark, 'I've been waiting for your call. Annabel tells me you're interested in working for me.'

'Yes, I am.' And as I said it out loud for the first time, I realised I was very interested in working for Mark, for reasons other than the money: now that I talked to him, now that it was real, I started to feel the first faint stirrings of arousal.

'Well, why don't we meet over coffee? You can't possibly consider working for me until you've *met* me.' He named an exclusive hotel bar and I was to meet him there after work tomorrow. The following day, at lunchtime, I had my nails done, a pedicure and a blow-dry, hoping that my credit cards would cover the cost and they did – just about.

Mark was waiting for me in the bar: his appearance

matched his voice. He tall, well-groomed, wearing head-to-toe black Armani. Although his face was young and unlined, his hair was shot through with a dark, steely grey, like George Clooney. This lent him an air of authority that had me instantly at ease with him. The hand he held out to greet me was manicured, and the cheek that brushed mine when he air-kissed me was soft, but peppered with the beginnings of a five-o'-clock shadow.

Mark drank mineral water while I sipped on a long herbal tea. As we spoke, he outlined the terms and conditions. His polite, well-to-do voice was at odds with the explicit nature of his words.

'The fee is $200 an hour. That includes straight sex, oral or a hand job. Whether you do anything else is up to you: most of my girls charge $500 for anal penetration, threesomes or a little light bondage – you can say no to any of these extras. They're optional.' I nodded, trying to keep my expression neutral, although the twin thrills of money and sex were turning me on, big time. 'You provide your own condoms, lingerie and any other extras you need. I take fifty per cent of whatever you make,' Mark continued. 'If the client gives you a tip, it's all yours. I vet all my clients and have an elite network of men who use my services. They expect discretion and an immaculate appearance. You will call me once when the client picks you up and then every ninety minutes until you finish the job.'

As Mark spoke, I lost myself in a reverie of sucking cock in expensive hotel rooms; the thought of having a rich man's dick between my lips, making him come, was a thrill: I was going to give them the best blow-jobs money could buy.

'You'll need to be an actress. You need to pretend you're having a good time even if you're not. But if you do get horny – which can happen – you must never lose sight of the fact he's paying you to pleasure *him*. He's in charge: you do it the way your client wants. Think you can handle it?' I nodded.

'Well, that's the first part of your interview over,' said Mark, discreetly settling the tab with the bartender and leaving a ten-dollar tip. 'Shall we go upstairs?' Annabel hadn't warned me that the interview would involve a practical as well as the theory, but of course, it was obvious: Mark would need to sleep with me if he was going to hire me. From his point of view, there was no point paying a girl a grand a night if she was going to lie motionless and cold.

I nodded, scared that my voice would waver and betray the nerves (and arousal) I was feeling. I wanted to keep this as cool and businesslike as I could. A porter called the hotel lift and we headed for the tenth floor. It was just the two of us in the lift: Mark's expensive aftershave filled the tiny space and made my head swim. 'If you come to work for me, you'll get to know this building,' he said as the lift climbed the floors. 'I keep three rooms here all year round. Clients often prefer a neutral space and if the room is included in the booking it won't show up on a credit card bill. And with the best will in the world, not all of my girls have apartments that are the standard my clients have come to expect.' We walked down a dimly lit corridor to a white door: Mark took a key from his pocket and ushered me in. 'Plus, I need somewhere appropriate to audition girls. Make yourself comfortable.'

The room was fashionably furnished in black-and-white furniture with a chessboard carpet and a huge, gold rococo mirror hanging directly over the bed. While I took in my surroundings, Mark disappeared into the bathroom. I began to undress, anticipation growing and bubbling. By the time Mark came back I was down to my lingerie, stockings and heels.

'No,' Mark stood in the bathroom doorway, looked disapproving. 'Always undress your client first – or allow him to undress – before you take your own clothes off. It gives you more control, and he can make himself hard while you strip for him.'

So I perched on a chair and watched while Mark took off his clothes, folding them neatly on the back of a sculpted black leather chaise longue. Naked, he was magnificent: broad, tall, gym-honed but rock solid, he had the physique of a quarterback footballer. His tight, well-developed chest had a smattering of black hair: he was the most masculine man I'd ever seen. He must have been twice my weight: I thought of how it would feel to have those chunky arms wrapped around my waist, supporting me as he fucked me from behind, and the faint stirrings of sexual arousal grew into something stronger. Mark walked across the room, displaying a short but thick dick, slightly darker in colour than the rest of his body. As he sank back into the pillows of the bed, I focused on that dick.

Okay, I thought. I'm going to use my mouth to make you hard, harder than you've ever been before. Then I'm going to get on top of you and fuck you until you beg me to let you come. I tried to ignore the damp patch forming in my panties; this was about Mark's pleasure, not mine.

Sure that Mark was comfortable, I stood in front of him, dressed in black underwear, French knickers, garter belt and a half-cup bra threaded with baby-pink ribbons: this was my favourite lingerie. It made my alabaster skin look like marble, and the pale pink of the ribbons matched the colour of my nipples and pussy. I let his eyes travel over my body for a few seconds. He nodded his approval, as though sizing up a new piece of expensive furniture or a car. His gaze was steely but his dick stayed limp. Time for the strip show, I thought.

Instead of undoing my bra by the clasp, I let the shoulder straps down one by one. I pulled first one breast, then the other, out of the cups. My pink nipples resting on the edge of the fabric, hardening and darkening as they reacted to the air-conditioning in the room and my own mounting desire. I turned my back to him and slipped the French knickers over my hips, giving him a chance to check out the butt I'd spent so long honing to perfection in the gym and admire the garter belt around my waist, keeping my sheer stockings in place. I stepped out of the silk underwear and then bent down to touch my toes and parted my legs, looking at Mark upside-down from between my thighs. His face gave nothing away and neither did his dick. Still no hard-on! With one lightning-fast movement I unclasped my bra and removed it, holding to one side before letting it fall to the floor. Slowly, I turned around, so that Mark could see my naked breasts: their rapid rise and fall, in time with my breath that had grown fast and shallow, betraying my body's response to what was happening. I put one foot on the bed, legs splayed, giving Mark his first glimpse of the pubic hair I'd had waxed into a red flaming flash, like a lightning bolt.

'Natural redhead,' he said, and although his voice was neutral and his mind was still clearly in pimp mode, his body was finally telling a different story. Although Mark's hands remained motionless by his sides, his dick was finally starting to stir, rising up from his body until it was bolt upright, almost parallel with his stomach. His exposed balls were smooth, round, the same tawny colour as his hard-on. I licked my lips as it doubled in length before my eyes: I might have thought his dick was short at first glance, but fully erect it was the biggest I'd ever seen. I knew that my wet pussy would have no problems accommodating it, but would I ever be able to fit it all in my mouth? I'd have fun trying, that was for sure. My own body responded in kind, the first droplets of juice forming in my pussy and my labia swelling and darkening in preparation to be wrapped around Mark's erection.

I made to remove my garter belt, but Mark gave another command. 'Keep it on,' he said, in a low growl. Happy to obey, I crawled across the huge hotel bed, naked but for my sheer, seamed hose and garter. Gently, I parted Mark's legs and knelt beneath them, inches away from his dick. It quivered and bounced in anticipation. I took a deep breath and lowered my head to kiss it. He'd trimmed his pubic hair, making things easier for me. I wrapped my lips around the head of his penis and with my tongue gently teased back his foreskin to reveal a healthy, bright pink tip underneath. This trick would have most guys begging me to take it all in my mouth: Mark remained inscrutable. The less response he showed, the hotter it made me feel.

I slid my mouth slowly down the shaft of his dick, tracing my tongue around every vein, every pulsating inch of skin. He was so big that to take the last couple of inches inside my mouth, I had to bear down as hard as I could: the tip of his penis banged against the back of my throat: I knew from experience that this was the point where an orgasm could often take a guy by surprise, the intense stimulation tripping him into a climax right there inside me. But not Mark. I should have known he'd be more of a challenge.

Pulling back a little, I moved up and down his hard-on, my whole mouth travelling the length of his dick. My nipples brushed against the hair of his strong thighs, and I shook my tits, knowing this would stimulate them even more, and knowing that the harder and darker they got the more impressive they would look when I pulled my head up from Mark's dick and arched my back, ready to straddle him. I wanted him to pull them, grab them, squeeze them hard. I wanted for him to be incapable of keeping his hands away from them. But he remained still, his trembling hard-on the only evidence of how turned on he was.

A couple of telltale jerks of his pelvis let me know that Mark would come if I carried on giving him head, and I certainly didn't want to have him reach his orgasm without showing him what else I could do. Using one hand to gently tug his balls, I slowly pulled away from his dick and knelt with my legs either side of his cock, using my free hand to part my pink pussy lips which hovered an inch or two away, so near and yet so far from allowing him to penetrate me. I let him feast his eyes on my body for a second or two, watching his face for signs of excitement. Nothing. Didn't this guy ever lose control? I was putting in a performance that would have most fellas fighting back an orgasm. I let go of his balls and reached over to the bedside table, where I'd placed a condom.

'Good girl' said Mark, eyeing the little foil square appreciatively. With one quick motion I opened it and rolled it on to his cock, smoothing it down with my hands, repeating the motion, stroking it and daring him to moan in pleasure. Instead, he maintained the cool detachment of the potential customer browsing in a store.

I had to bite my lip to stop myself sighing and crying out with frustration. By this point during sex I would usually have a man's hands roaming, exploring and awakening my body: I'd have had lips licking my pussy, a finger probing my clit, breasts massaged by greedy hands, a thumb up my arse and a tongue in most of those places – a body pressed against mine. Mark had laid a single finger on me, but I was as turned on as though a million hands were manipulating every erogenous zone I had.

Once I was sure the condom was on comfortably, I lowered my pussy down on to Mark's erection. I was so wet, his penis slid in effortlessly: he couldn't help but notice how much I wanted him. I wondered if it was bad form or good for a whore to get as much – more even – out of the experience than her client. On the one hand, it was gonna make the guy feel good about himself, give him a massive ego boost. On the other, I had to stay in control. This was not ordinary sex: this was not about chasing my own orgasm. This was about showing what I could do. This was about making him come. This was about proving I was such a good fuck that I deserved to be a grand-a-night hooker.

I bounced up and down on Mark's cock, slowly at first and then in time with the thrusts his own hips made. I pulled his knee up to my chest, altering the angle of his hips so that his dick went deeper and harder into my cunt. I pushed down on to him, my whole weight bearing down on his hard-on, then rose up so that only the tip of his penis was still inside me. I twisted my hips, swivelling from side to side, massaging his dick.

All the while I concentrated on his pleasure, hoping to defer my own. I had never, ever had an orgasm through penetration alone: I always needed a tongue, fingers or a toy on my clit to get there. I'd thought that up here, on top, I could control it. But as I straddled this strong, silent man, I felt a build-up of tension in my own pelvis that demanded to be released. My instinct was to bend down and kiss Mark, but in the back of my mind I had an idea that the whore's code forbade kissing. I should have taken notes last time I watched *Pretty Woman*. Instead, I had to settle for licking my fingers and pinching my breasts, pretending that it was his lips on my nipples.

And that did it. Finally, Mark's impassive face broke into a frown, then a smile, and he let out a whimper that told me just what effect I was having on him. Once he'd started there was no stopping him: his hands were all over me, one finger on my tits, the other between my lips. I sucked on his finger. He moaned a little louder. I bit down on it. He grunted, an animal sound that sent a shiver down my spine.

With that, I forgot about client/call-girl etiquette and I let my body tell me what to do.

Now that Mark had lost control, he totally abandoned himself to the rhythm of our fucking. His pubic bone was grinding against mine: the rasp of his bush grinding against my swollen clit was too much for me to bear, making me cry out. 'Fuck me!' I screamed, forgetting that Mark was supposed to be the one giving orders here. 'Fuck me! Fuck me!' I almost sobbed the words. Mark did fuck me, harder than ever. His body bucked, pushing his dick deep into me. I knew what I needed to get there, but it would mean putting my own pleasure before his. I forgot all about working for Mark, I forgot all about everything but the climax I needed, and I placed his thumb on my clitoris for a couple of seconds. That was all it took. I felt the familiar electric current starting in my pelvis and radiating out through by body, white-hot points of light erupting in my clit, my arse, my tits, and sending a tell-tale blush across my cheeks and chest. I closed my eyes, riding out the last few seconds of my orgasm. My pussy continued its rapid contractions, a series of tiny squeezes as fast as the flutter of butterfly wings around his cock.

Mark came seconds later. Eyes flickering, he lay back on the hotel bed, his whole body making one, two, three huge tremors as he lost control of himself at last. 'Oh God! Oh God!' he shouted. His hair remained immaculate but his deadpan features twisted and sweat beaded on his forehead.

As my orgasm subsided, I remained frozen to the spot, appalled by what I'd done. I'd broken the golden rule and put my own pleasure before that of my client. I eased myself off Mark's diminishing erection and removed the condom, using a tissue to wipe him clean before disposing of it in the bathroom. I splashed cold water on my face and examined myself in the mirror. Dishevelled hair, pink cheeks, sparkling eyes: the climax I'd just had was written all over my features.

'You fucking fool,' I said to my reflection. 'You've blown your big chance to get out of debt,' I told myself.

And there was another voice in the back of my head, saying, 'And you'll never fuck Mark again now, either.' But that was the least of my worries.

I wrapped myself in a hotel bathrobe and returned to the bedroom, where Mark had draped a sheet over himself. He had also raided the minibar and handed me a glass of champagne. On the pillow was a fold of $50 bills. I counted them: two grand. It must be a pay-off.

'To cover your expenses for the evening,' he said. And then, just what I was dreading, 'Time for your debriefing. You do know what went wrong there, don't you?'

I hung my head. 'I'm sorry,' I said. 'I tried to keep my cool, but you felt so good . . .' I bit back the tears.

'I've been doing this for fifteen years and you're certainly the most remarkable first fuck I've ever had,' he said, with the detachment of a man mulling over a business decision. 'Most of my girls take weeks of practise to develop the sensual confidence that comes naturally to you. Annabel, for example, had to take lessons from some of my more senior girls just to get her oral skills up to scratch. But you, Kerry, you're different. You just enjoy sex too much: you're not a natural escort, and with that attitude, you'll never be the working girl I'm looking for. It's a shame, really: you're very attractive, and clearly extremely skilled, but I just can't trust you not to put your own satisfaction before that of your client.'

'So I'm not hired because I'm too good?' I said, fingers closing around the cash Mark had given me before he demanded it back. I was bitterly disappointed but at least I had enough money to pay my rent for the next month.

'I didn't say you weren't hired,' said Mark, and topped up my champagne. 'Just that I couldn't trust you with my clients. I have another position I'd like to offer. The arrangement I have in mind is rather more exclusive. You will be fucking one specific, very exacting customer. He'll want you for two nights a week, plus the occasional weekend. He pays very well.'

I was confused but intrigued. 'Who is he?' I asked. Mark leaned forward and kissed me for the first time, peppery stubble rasping against my cheek. He tasted of champagne.

'Didn't I say?' he said, eyes twinkling. 'It's me.'

ASH

This confession about a beautiful stranger has a fabulous twist in the tale: I'll never forget gasping with shock – and, okay, arousal – when Nina told me the story of the night she picked up a stranger who was not all he appeared to be.

The moral of this story? Sometimes the unexpected can be even more delicious than the anticipated.

Put me in a room full of men of all shapes, sizes and colours, and I'll go for the pale and interesting skinny boy every time. Why do willowy, androgynous men get me weak at the knees and wet between the legs? Time and time again, the men I draw to me, the men to whom I call across crowded bars with nothing more than a smile, the boys whose lips wrap around my nipples, whose heads rest in my lap and whose cocks I crave, are beautiful, delicate, finely chiselled creatures. Apart from their looks, they have one thing in common: they have the stamina to go on, and on, all night. They might look reedy, but these slips of lads can fuck for hours and they're always eager to learn more about making me happy.

And what do they see in me? I couldn't be *less* androgynous: I'm proud of my big, round tits that are still pert, the nipped in, hourglass waist that looks as if I'm wearing a corset and my generous arse and wide, sensual hips. Couple that with my long, dark hair that reaches in snaky curls down my back and my olive skin, like a year-round tan: no wonder my last lover called me his Spanish guitar and worshipped my curves.

I know where to find my boys. Dingy little gigs at indie clubs, at university and college bars, hanging around in grimy pubs, they come out at night, social vampires who don't surface during the day. They're usually too shy and sensitive to come and talk to me, so I smile sweetly and fix my eyes on them. The double-barrelled attack of lipstick on my pillow lips and mascara-lashed eyes never fails. Once they know that they'll get a warm welcome from me, they'll approach. And I don't let them go until I've got what I want – and I always get my man.

When I meet Ash, he ticks all the usual boxes. An unsigned band's playing in a town-centre club, and I see him as soon as I walk in: standing in the corner near the bar, nursing a neat whisky and dressed in a sharp pinstriped suit teamed with battered trainers and a baggy shirt and tie. The trousers hang loose from his snaky hips. I like that a lot.

He's tall – about six foot – and his dark brown hair is teased and slicked into a shiny quiff, forties-style. He has dark, straight eyebrows, not too thick, framing pale green eyes.

His delicate jawline and high cheekbones make him look half-boy, half-cat, and his upper lip pouts slightly over the bottom one. There's a slight sneer about his mouth. I like that too. A challenge, I think.

But I'm wrong. For once, the guy looks at me – making it clear that he's the one making the decision here. I hold his gaze: I don't do demure. For the length of an entire song, our eyes are locked. In that two-and-a-half minute period, I run through a string of sexual positions I want to force his skinny little body into. That sulky lip wrapped around my nipple, that bony back arching in pleasure as he clambers on top and fucks me. Oh yes. I've got lots of ideas about what to do with this one. I decide to move matters along a little – maybe he is too shy to make the first move after all.

I walk up to the bar. 'Hey,' I say, gesturing to his nearly empty glass and hazarding a guess at his drink of choice. 'Jack Daniels?' I was right. It's *always* Jack Daniels.

'Thanks.' He doesn't smile back but he takes the drink all right. Well, that's students for you. 'I'm Ash,' he says, holding out his hand for me to shake. 'Nina,' I say simply, holding his hand for a fraction of a second. I saw the chunky silver name bracelet on his wrist suggesting a cool, camp ironic touch – or a sense of humour I'm just not picking up on in person.

There's an awkward silence, which I'm not sure how to handle. His signals are all over the place: staring at me, then sulking when I get up close. I can tell he's interested. Light hits the skin on his cheek and I see how soft it is. Oh, he's very young. He needs me to take charge. So I just come right out and say it.

'I want your mouth on my tit,' I say, and expect him to run away. If he does, I'm gonna be really pissed off, and I'm gonna have to head straight for the ladies and bring myself off because there's something about this one that's got me extremely hot.

Ash takes a step closer so that I can smell his breath and the lemony scent he's wearing. He smells fresh and clean. Nice. Slowly, he stretches his hand towards me. Although the built-in support of my halter top makes it complete guesswork, his long fingers locate my nipple instantly. I admire his hunter instinct.

'I don't know if I can fit all that big, juicy tit in my mouth,' he whispers, knuckles brushing the hardening nub of my nipple, and his voice is smooth and soft, 'But we're going to have fun trying.'

We're out through the club doors in seconds, and for once there's a taxi right outside, the orange For Hire light a beacon, making my journey home to bed so much quicker. I grunt my address to the taxi driver and Ash and I fall into the back seat, tangled up in each other.

He comes to kiss me and his kisses are urgent, masculine, searching, his tongue probing my mouth the way I want his cock to when we get home. He kisses expertly, leaving no corner of my mouth unexplored. I feel a dull ache of wanting between my legs and my confidence in this boy's experience grows.

I dig my fingers into the hollows of his arse. I'm desperate to free his dick, I can't wait to see his cock. What subtle hue will it have? How thick? How long? I pull back and check out his colouring. His mouth bears traces of my scarlet lipstick. A marked man. Pale skin, dark hair: I picture a pale, smooth, pink-tipped hard-on jutting proudly from beneath a generous jet-black bush the same colour as his eyebrows, with that little fuse of hair tracing a line from cock to navel that I'm so crazy about. I'm so impatient: I can't wait and I won't wait, and the sooner I see it, the less likely I am to be disappointed.

But Ash wriggles away whenever my fingers make a play for his zipper, and he grabs my wrists, forces my hands on my breasts, and the two of us move as one, massaging and kneading my flesh. He's clearly mesmerised by my tits, and buries his face in them. So I'm happy to make my cleavage the focus of attention in the taxi, and save his cock for later.

We speed through rainy London streets, the driver turning a blind eye to this tangle of limbs in the back of his cab. Fifteen minutes into the journey I'm so stoked that frankly I could fuck Ash here and now, at forty miles an hour – it wouldn't be the first time – but the condoms are in my bag and I'm not fumbling around for them in the dark, spoiling the moment.

We arrive back at mine and Ash almost pushes me up the steps to the front door of my building. Standing one step below me, we're at level height, and his breath on my neck and his tongue exploring the sensitive skin just behind my ear (how did he know that's my weak spot?) is a real distraction and it takes an age to find my keys. When I finally locate my housekey Ash slides his hands between my legs, just resting that gentle hand against the cotton of my panties, which are getting wetter by the second. He doesn't move his hand, just holds it still so I can feel the pulse of his fingers mark time with the throbbing of my vulva. It's so powerful it's all I can do to get the key in the door, and I feel warmth on my shoulder as Ash laughs a husky laugh, delighted that his teasing has the desired effect.

And then we're in the hallway, and through my door into my studio apartment – with the blinds pulled down – and finally this beautiful boy and I are alone together in a room dominated by the bed. I'm sorry, but his last excuse to keep that dick in his pants has just gone. I'm about to tell him this when he pulls me to him and we kiss again, standing face to face. I stand on tiptoe so that our pelvises are level, and I push my hips into his crotch and . . . I can't feel a hard-on. Now I'm confused because in my experience, when a young man kisses this passionately, there's a fully erect cock waiting for me. I can't have read the signals all wrong, can I? We pull away, a string of our mingled saliva linking our lips together and I see the naked lust on his face and know that he wants me. If he sees my baffled expression, he doesn't say anything.

'Now,' he says, 'about those big, beautiful tits,' and he pulls at the stretchy material of my top, fingers finding my most sensitive areas with an uncanny, magnetic instinct. While he's doing this, I reach behind my neck and undo the ties of my halterneck so that when I let the ribbons go – slap! my tits are freed and my pups are out and proud. They're spherical, bouncy and brown against the white cotton of my top. I look down. Fuck me! Even I've never seen my nipples this erect. They're hard as diamonds, standing to attention, impatiently waiting for his tongue.

Sure enough, he starts sucking on them, hungrily, greedily. Few men really know how to kiss a nipple, but Ash does, covering his teeth with his lips and administering tiny bites that hurt just enough, teasing me with his tongue and not quite touching them, then suddenly sucking *hard* and pulling his head back so that my soft, round tits are pulled out by the force of his mouth, morphing into pyramids that return to their natural round shape when he lets them go. Then he lightly slaps my breasts, side to side, his green eyes like saucers as they sway in two large teardrops. The feel of his skin on mine is a wake-up call to every nerve ending in my body. No one has ever done this to me before and I'm thinking, 'Why not?' as my breasts swell and the colour deepens to a delicious dark pink. If this sight doesn't have his dick sitting up and begging for me, then I don't know what will.

Now that he's seen my tits, Ash can't wait to see the rest of me and he unpeels me like a piece of ripe fruit. He pulls my gypsy skirt down around my waist and makes light work of my panties, tearing them off me. I'm sprawled on my futon, naked apart from my sandals and a halter-neck top tangled around my waist, ribbons tickling and teasing the sides of my thighs. Ash pinches my left nipple, then the right and as the heat floods through my body I wonder if I'm going to come through having my breasts fondled alone. I am on fire with longing. I rewind all my past sexual experiences: nope. Never been hot for anyone like this before.

Ash throws his suit jacket on the floor and kicks off his shoes and socks, but other than that, he's still fully clothed. He's still wearing his tie, which is actually kind of horny – it makes the contrast with my nakedness even sexier. But that's all got to change, because I want to come so badly that I know the only way stave off my orgasm is to take time out and concentrate on pleasuring Ash for a while.

'Ash,' I murmur, tugging at his tie. 'Baby,' and I smile a sleepy, sexy smile which he returns, bright-eyed and panting with lust. 'Let me return the favour.' And this is when he starts to look nervous, but I don't buy this shy-boy shit: anyone who can play a woman's body like that without even touching her pussy isn't some inexperienced little boy. So what's the play-acting for? But I play along. 'C'mon,' and I beckon him over with a red-nailed finger. 'Let me undress you. I want to see what you look like.'

He stays where he is, and slides off his tie. Then, achingly slowly, the little cunt-tease unbuttons his shirt, turning his back to me so I can't see his chest and torso. I'm aching to find out whether he's got that little line of hair on his stomach running down to his pubes, and what colour his nipples are. But I want to check out his arse, too; oh, what a dilemma!

'I want to see you,' I beg. He looks over his shoulder, unsmiling, and lets his shirt drop to the floor. His back is a criss-cross of slender, athletic muscle tautening on a lean body, just the way I like it: no spare flesh at all – I'll provide the curves, thank you very much. Again, I look down at my own rippling body and imagine what it'll feel like when his light, bony hips grind against my own soft pelvis. He unbuckles his belt and drops his trousers – he's not wearing any boxers – to reveal the most beautiful, hairless, tight little arse I've seen in a long, long time. His legs are lean, too. He bends down to kick off his trousers and sinew ripples along his legs, like a swimmer gliding through a pool. I can't help myself, and my hand goes between my legs in anticipation of the erection he's about to show me. He turns around slowly and –

What the fuck?

My first thought is – this is some childish, not-very-funny-at-all joke – that he's tucked his dick between his legs. But as my eyes travel up the body before me I notice that there really is nothing between his legs, there's a very subtle swelling of the hips and there, at the top of the hairless chest, there are two delightfully tiny little tits, with huge pink nipples sitting up and begging for my attention. I've never seen anything like those nipples – at least the same size as the whole tit, even as I watch them hardening into two rose-pink puffed-up petals.

'I thought you knew . . .' Ash's voice falters and now of course I can't believe that I didn't know. And I have a choice here. I can either get really, really fucking angry, and throw her out into the night, or I can listen to my body, because even as I'm finding my eyes stuck on Ash's jutting hipbones and dark, untamed bush, I'm thinking – you know what? This girl is *hot*.

Ash's confidence is on the wane now. She can tell I'm hesitating and I know that she still wants me. Like, really wants me. And that's what makes my mind up. Because if there's one thing gets me off, it's the look in someone's eyes when they've seen me and they want me. I laugh, at my own naïveté as much as anything else, and it breaks the tension.

'You wanted to return the favour?' she says, falteringly, and walks over to where I'm sitting, so that the black hair on her mound is level with my eyes.

'I've never been with a woman,' I tell her, and it's true, but this wiry little bitch is half-boy half-girl and I want her all the more for it. I breathe in her musk and it makes me dizzy with lust. I reach up and flick that nipple with my thumb and forefinger, check it's real. It glows under my touch. Oh, baby – it's real all right.

She comes closer, puts her bush right in my face and while I'm thinking about sliding my tongue into that tuft of darkness, she slides down my body, so I can feel her pussy juices moisten my own tits, and when her head is just above mine, she offers me one of those cute little boobs. I wrap my own soft lips around her nipple, but her tits are so tiny I can fit the whole thing in my mouth and still have room left over to suck at the skin around her breasts. I get greedy. I've got her tit so far in my mouth that I'm close to gagging on her nipple, which almost nuzzles at the back of my throat.

Then we're lying back on the sofa, kissing, really deep-throat kissing, and instinct or force of habit has me groping between her legs, searching for a hard-on to guide into my hungry slit. Of course all I feel is Ash's own soft, wet sex, surrounded by her pubic hair which is surprisingly downy and soft. My hands travel up and down the inside of her thighs instead and suddenly I'm the nervous one. I can think of a million ways to have fun with a hard-on, but my experience of getting another woman off is another thing. I needn't worry though: Ash likes what I'm doing: her nipples are harder as they rub against my own tits, which make slapping sounds as our bodies collide, and I can hear a faint kissing noise as our two soaking pussies rub together.

Ash pulls away, tucks a curl behind my ear and grins at me. 'God, you're bewitching,' she says, in that gravelly voice too deep for a girl and too high for a boy. She's pretty bewitching herself. She lies on top of me on the sofa, we're welded together, and spend a couple of minutes snogging, just letting the sexual tension build up. I'm buying myself time, too: building up the confidence to put my face where I know she wants me to. The longer we stay holding each other, the more I want to put my face in that muff, slide my tongue inside her and make her come. The more I think about this, the more urgent it seems, until desire overtakes shyness and I've *got* to taste her. I flip that long tall body around 180 degrees so she's the one on her back now. I turn my back on her and straddle her tummy, parting her legs with my arms and breathing in before I dive. My arse, which I hope she likes the look of, is up on her chest.

I delve, voraciously. She smells good and she tastes amazing, too. Her clit is like a little cock: erect and sensitive, I can feel it growing harder with my every touch. She's moaning behind me, repeating everything she says twice.

'Nina . . . Nina . . . fuck, yeah . . . fuck, yeah . . .'

And then I feel what I want to happen, a sharp, delving tongue parting my arse cheeks and making its way to my own pussy. Because of the angle, she has to stimulate my clit with her hands, and she does this beautifully, holding it just lightly enough between her thumb and forefinger, gently tugging while her tongue swirls around my lips and eventually penetrates me.

We fall into a rhythm, swaying, sucking, fucking. I can tell she's going to come, because her whole body tenses, and her tongue hardens and stops moving. No one can concentrate on giving and receiving this level of pleasure simultaneously. But her fingers stay near my clit, and this tiny tug, combined with her moans is propelling *me* close to orgasm. It takes all my sexual stamina to concentrate on Ash and not relax into my own climax, but I keep rocking and using my tongue to get her there.

'Fuuuuuuuuuuuuuuuuuuuuuuuuuuuuck . . .'

Ash is coming hard. My tongue sucks her clit and I can feel her body rock under mine. As she comes, she loses control and pulls really hard on my own clitoris, probably harder than she meant to. It finally tips me over the edge. The tension is finally released and I'm bucking like a horse, lost in my own pleasure as her sweet juices trickle out of her and spill down her pink crack, where I lick them up.

My legs are shaking. I summon the energy to roll over on to my back. Quick as a flash, Ash crawls up my body, and sinks into my open arms. I trace her eyebrows with a fingertip, push back the quiff that's fallen over her eyes.

'You got me here under false pretences,' I say, frowning.

'You still wish I was a man?' she says, in a husky drawl that's so sexy I'm almost ready to go again. I breathe in the smell of her that fills the room.

'No,' I say, stroking her breasts, and I mean it. 'You've been a revelation. I never knew dickless sex could be so intense,' I confess.

'You call that intense?' said Ash. 'Wait till you come to mine and I fuck you hard with my strap-on.'

'Oh dear,' I say. 'I'm not very good at waiting.' And I call us a cab to Ash's place.

ALL TOMORROW'S PARTIES

We all dream of meeting a mysterious stranger and being seduced into his world. But how many of us would be brave enough to abandon ourselves to a dark, brooding artist we'd only just met? The eighteen-year-old ingénue told me this story about the chance meeting with a man who changed her life and turned her on to sex. It's a seriously sexy tale about that point where you realise you might get in over your head . . . and you decide to jump right in anyway.

When I was young, growing up in the suburbs, all I ever wanted was two things: to dance and to live in London. Three days after my eighteenth birthday I realised both ambitions when I was awarded a place at the prestigious London Dance Academy. I received a grant to spend on *pointe* shoes and leotards: I blew the lot on wild clothes, ultra-fashionable garments to be worn after dark, as soon as I arrived.

I threw myself into all that London had to offer,

burning the candle at both ends. I spent as much time dancing in clubs at night as I did training at the *barre* during the day. This was no time to be shy. Within a couple of months, every club promoter and doorman in the West End knew my name and face: sixties-style long blonde hair cut with a blunt fringe across the eyes that were worn with loads of eyeliner was my trademark look. In the dark of the nightclub, I stood out, a ghost under the spotlights. My new-found friends from the academy and I could turn an empty dance floor into a hotspot heaving with bodies within the duration three-minute house track. We had free entry into any underground club we wanted, and never paid for drinks. Not that we drank much: as dancers, we had to keep our bodies in shape.

If you think my nocturnal existence was seedy, you couldn't be more wrong: if anything, there was an innocence about those early months in the big smoke. For me, clubbing was never about sex: it was about the music. More often than not, the best dancers are gay, and any bump and grind would be to show off our skills rather than for sexual gratification. I looked confident on the dancefloor, but the way I swung my hips to music disguised a surprising lack of sexual experience. I'd always put dancing before boyfriends, and at eighteen, had yet to lose my virginity. And I was in no hurry: I was too busy falling in love with life to think about sex. The people I met in clubs were not just dancers, but writers, film-makers, artists of every kind. Most of them had been in London for years, and when I wasn't dancing I was listening to their stories of the city before my time, of other places they'd visited, wild parties they'd thrown. They loved having such an eager audience: I soaked up their stories like a sponge.

One night I caught the attention of an edgy-looking guy at a jazz club in some grimy East End basement. He was as dark as I was blonde, with jet-black eyes, unshaven, with a wild mop of tousled black hair. And for some reason I wanted to run my fingers through it, but I didn't. He was tall and skinny and wore tight-fitting black clothes that hinted at a wiry body underneath. He stood like a dancer: erect, composed, elegant. He walked up to me and introduced himself as David.

'I'm an artist,' he said. 'I'm looking for a muse. Would you like to be my muse?' No small talk; just the bare bones. His directness was disarming. 'There's a party on at my house. Want to come?' Though totally out of character for me, it didn't even cross my mind not to go with him.

'Sure,' I said. 'The night's still young. And anyway, you can't really dance to jazz. Let's get out of here.' And I followed him out of the basement, up a staircase and into the night.

On the street, David turned to me. He had to bend

right down to talk to me. So close I could smell his breath, sweet and salty on the cold night air. He looked younger than he had in the club: early twenties, maybe.

'What's your name?' he said.

'Charlie,' I told him.

'Well, Charlie-girl,' he said, giving me a sexy snaggle-toothed smile that made my stomach flip over. 'Let me introduce you to my friends.'

He lived in a building unlike anything I'd ever seen. Huge and draughty, it looked more like a disused ware-house than a block of flats. We accessed his floor via four flights of a rickety fire escape to a balcony that looked out across the twinkling London skyline.

'What kind of artist are you to be able to afford a place like *this*?' I asked, and immediately regretted it, thinking how uncool and gauche that must have sounded.

David threw back his head and laughed, revealing a seductive crooked smile: his tongue darted between his lips like a lizard's. Looking at his mouth made me blush. I felt the telltale pink patches appear on my otherwise porcelain skin, and felt a vague, unfamiliar stirring between my legs.

'Oh,' he said, 'You'll find out about my art soon enough.'

He turned his key in the door and led me into another world. The place was vast. There was no other word for it. You could easily have fit my parents' suburban semi inside it three times over. It was a high-ceilinged loft space, with whitewashed brick on the walls, and almost no furnishings other than a stainless-steel kitchen, huge couches and a few battered old armchairs scattered about the place. But the walls! The walls were covered in fantastic, multicoloured images on huge white canvases, twenty feet square. The paintings consisted of bold swirls of paint that seemed to writhe and whirl in front of my eyes in tangled, curved and sensual shapes.

'This is your work?' I asked David.

'It's *our* work,' he said, and gestured to the dozen or so people who lay draped along the sofas. I smiled shyly at the exotic creatures: a man in a harlequin suit, a stunning Latina girl wearing only a pair of panties, two women in men's suits, a black man clad in head-to-toe leather. There were also a few guys and girls wearing regular clothes. 'These are my collaborators. This is The Collective,' he said, with a sweep of the arm that took all of them in at once.

'And this,' he said, placing his hands on my shoulders and steering me to face his friends, 'Is Charlie-girl, my beautiful ingénue. She dances like an angel.' His words flattered me, making me nervous, but I could hardly hear him over the roar of my heartbeat, blood closer to the surface of my skin than ever before. It was the first time he touched me and even though it was only his hands on my shoulders, through my clothes, I felt that I had suddenly been brought to life. I used my body to dance, all day every day, I thought, but I'd never been so aware of it as I am right now.

'Hi,' I said, suddenly dumbstruck in the face of all these stylish people.

'Let me get you a drink,' said David, and then, sensing that I was a little overwhelmed, with a tender glance added, 'It's okay. They're cool.'

I stayed up all night, listening to their stories but reluctant to share any of my own, such as they were. Everyone had so much life experience that I couldn't compete: Katya, the woman in the mannish suit, made everyone laugh with tales of a sex club she'd been to in her native Ukraine. Jem, the guy in the harlequin suit, was camp and witty with a barbed comment for anyone who took themselves too seriously. The Latina girl in only her underwear turned out to be called Rosario: she remained silent, and her function seemed to be doubling up as a pillow for anyone who needed a soft place to rest. At one point I saw Jem lay his head on her breasts, nearly asleep. Even my dance friends would have found this a little weird but I tried not to bat an eyelid: I didn't want to blow my cool. These confident, arty people were the kind I'd always dreamt I'd hang out with – the whole point of my coming to London. If only

I could think of something to say that would make them want to invite me back. I felt very young and inexperienced amongst all these great people.

But things changed when someone walked over to the stereo and selected a CD. David had a great music system, with hidden speakers that flooded stadium-quality sound throughout the airy loft. The tune was hard house, with a strong beat and rushing sweeps of melody, the kind that just compels dancers to move, instructs us, takes us over. At last, I didn't have to talk. I had finally found a language I could understand, communicate in. Without thinking I got up and started to sway. The song built to a crescendo and I surrendered to it, throwing shapes, grinding my hips, eyes closed, feeling nothing but the music.

When I opened my eyes, everyone had fallen silent. All eyes were on me. I was used to this attention when I danced. Suddenly confident, I sashayed over to Jem and offered him my hand, inviting him to accompany me on my impromptu dance floor. Once he was up, everyone joined in. All except David, who looked at me with a totally new expression: hungry, almost wolf-like. Again, my body was in a state of alertness that was alien to me. I danced for David's benefit, but he didn't join me, and I hadn't the nerve to ask him.

Eventually I collapsed, exhausted, on to a daybed by a vast window, while the others continued. David sat down next to me, and with one finger wiped the beads of sweat off my upper lip, then slid his finger in between my lips. Suddenly, all the confidence I had felt on the dance floor evaporated. I was nervous and shaking again.

'Look at you,' he said, stroking my long hair, skimming my breasts through the curtain of tresses, 'You're beautiful. Like a young Nico, or Marianne Faithfull.' I let out a giggle. Because his finger was on my lip, it came out as a gurgle. I blushed. No one had ever reduced me to a babbling fool like this before. He bent down and kissed me. It started soft and dry and then he slipped his tongue between my lips. He began exploring and gently nibbling at my mouth, probing, wanting to know me. I felt my body turn itself inside out with a twist of desire that took me so forcefully I was no longer sure I knew myself.

David let out a low moan. 'I could be hard and inside you now,' and with an expert movement, he slid his hand between my legs, his fingers exploring as deftly as his tongue had. I was shocked, not just because I'd never heard a guy voice his desires so explicitly before, but also by how wet my pussy was: I'd never felt like this before.

Things were moving way too fast for me. As David's fingers parted my pussy lips, he slid his thumb inside, hitting a tender spot no one had ever touched. Now it was his turn to be surprised.

'Charlie-girl,' he whispered, 'Don't tell me a chick who looks like you has never been . . .' He didn't finish his sentence, and he drew away from me, ending our kiss, leaving me relieved and frustrated all at the same time. He laid me down on his lap, stroking my hair. 'We're going to be amazing together, Charlie-girl,' he said.

The next thing I knew, it was morning. I woke up, blinking in the harsh city sunshine. Eyes dry, mascara clumping, everyone had gone home. Then I looked up. David was standing over me, covered in paint.

'I worked while you slept,' he said. 'You've inspired me. Want some coffee, Charlie-girl?'

'I'd love some,' I said, hoping I didn't look too awful.

He brought the coffee and sank on to the sofa with me. 'I'm always frank, Charlie,' he said. 'I want you so much it's killing me. But I don't want to rush things with you. I need to know if you're a virgin.' I nodded – what was the point of lying? – bowing my head so that I could hide my eyes behind my fringe.

'In that case, you're lucky,' said David, and there was a smile in his voice. 'You never have to have sex with some awful boy. I'm going to make you a woman today.'

He kissed me again, the dark stubble of his chin scuffing my lips. He tasted of fresh coffee and oil paint and the hands that slid under my dress and into my panties were flecked with paint. I kissed him back urgently, growing more confident and passionate by the second. Minutes later, I came up for air. David took one look at my face, exclaimed, 'Oh, poor baby!' and immediately vanished.

Mystified, I wondered what I had done for him to leave so suddenly. He reappeared after a couple of minutes, having shaved off his dark goatee of stubble. 'Your skin's like a rose petal's – easily bruised,' he murmured into my neck, 'I couldn't bear to rough you up. Well, not yet,' he said, and we both laughed. He fell on me. Once again his hands were under my minidress, hooking the panties that tied at the sides, sliding up and down my inner thighs but not quite touching me there, even as he pulled my knickers over my boots and threw them on the floor. Next, he whipped my dress over my head in one move. Now I was naked but for my suede knee boots, and David wore only a black T-shirt and jeans. I'd gone bra-less, as ever, and hoped my small breasts wouldn't be a disappointment. 'Oh, Christ,' moaned David, as one large hand travelled all over the front of my body. 'You're like a rosebud, a fresh oyster. I don't know whether to paint you or fuck you.'

I knew what *I* wanted, and gave him my answer by making a grab for his belt. Just like whenever I heard music, my body was taking over and I could hardly be held responsible for what would happen from this moment on. He removed his top and I gasped at the body that hovered over mine: he was thin but toned, every inch of his body defined by ripples of muscle and covered in fine, dark hair that made him look even more masculine and intense. Writhing under his touch, I somehow managed to free his buckle and threaded his black leather belt through the loops of his jeans. I could already see his erection straining under the restrictive tight black denim and as I unbuttoned his fly, we were both trembling. He slithered out of his jeans like a snake, and his cock was magnificent: smooth, the same pale biscuit colour as the rest of him, and trembling with anticipation, a fat tear of pre-cum oozing from its tip.

David knelt over me, sliding his hands over my hips, ribs, massaging and squeezing my tits until, I swear, they swelled to twice their normal size. Then he worked on my legs, kissing my inner thighs, working his way up towards my damp blonde bush. I wanted to cry out, but I didn't know the words to sum up these new feelings. I knew that I wanted something, but it was something I'd never experienced before, so how could I voice it?

He parted my legs. 'Now *that's* a very pretty picture,' he sighed, his breath a warm zephyr on my skin. 'So pink and wet,' and in the next second, that long pink tongue went to work on my clitoris, moving softly and smoothly around, tracing tiny circles, making me scream and clutch at David's hair as my desire mounted.

'I think you're ready for me, Charlie-girl,' David said.

Breathlessly, I nodded, and spread my legs as far as I could, my dancer's suppleness serving me well. With one finger he used the juices from my pussy to smoothly circle my clit. He propped himself up on one lean, muscular arm, hovered over me, looked down at my face and with a split-second of short, sharp pain, he entered me. The feeling of pain was immediately usurped by one of satisfaction the like of which I'd never known before. So this is what it's like to be fucked, I thought, as David drove his cock into me, filling me up again, and again, and again, pulling out to penetrate me all over again. I dug my fingers into his arse, driving him deeper and deeper and deeper, feeling the length of him inside me. The base of his dick was right where I needed it, rubbing away at my clit. I could feel something delicious bubbling up inside me. All the while, he was kissing me in that deep, intense, urgent way he had, stopping and starting: he'd draw away, sometimes to check the expression on my face, occasionally to pull at my nipples or take an entire tit in his sensual mouth. I closed my eyes, dizzy with pleasure, letting my body dance under David's touch. My orgasm, when it came, was my first; a swelling, followed by an eruption that made me cry out in pleasure and surprise. Shocked that my body was capable of something so intense, I lay beneath David, still pulsing with the aftershock of my climax. How had I lived without this for so long?

'I've made you mine, Charlie-girl,' said David. 'And now I'm going to paint you.' He withdrew from me, his proud erection twitching then submitting to the spasm of climax as he shot his spunk all over my tits, cooling my skin that was still on fire. I began to massage his white milk into me like body lotion, breathing in the fresh, but unfamiliar smell of it, working it down my tender flesh until it remained, glistening in my bush. I wanted to absorb David through my skin. He rolled around to my side and curved around me in the foetal position, wrapped around my waist. We lay there, neither of us speaking, David occasionally leaning into my body to inhale my skin, scent-marked with his come.

Eventually he broke the silence. 'You don't have to be anywhere today, do you?'

'No,' I said, and it was true, although I'd have broken any appointment to stay in David's apartment with him.

'Good,' he said, 'Because I'm already hard again at the thought of fucking you in all the different ways I know how.'

For rest of the weekend, he kept his promise. He gave me my second orgasm, my third, my fourth, my fifth and kept going until I lost count. Every time I thought I had gorged on pleasure, David would kiss me again and my body would be flooded with the same desire he'd unleashed the first seduction. When, on Sunday night, he finally put

me into a cab back to my apartment, he said goodbye
with a kiss that left me aching for our next encounter.

❧

On Monday in my dance class, I thought I'd be far too
exhausted to concentrate, but I danced with a renewed
sensuality that gave an unprecedented fluidity to my
movements. I was the envy of all my classmates as my
tutors praised me – surely I'd spent all weekend practising
to be this good, they gushed. I didn't let on that this kind
of dancing came with a new school of knowledge.

That night, fresh from the academy, I turned up to
David's apartment uninvited, and he welcomed me in as
though he'd been expecting me. He was still wearing his
skinny black uniform. He had me out of my own clothes
within seconds. For the first time since I'd moved to
London, I didn't go clubbing once that week.

❧

Saturday rolled around again – a week to the day since
I'd first made love with David. Already my virgin status
seemed a light year away. My newly discovered sexuality
was affecting more than my dancing. My confidence
increased by the day, my appetite for life grew, I wanted
to taste every experience and live every moment to the
full. So this Saturday, when I turned up to find The
Collective hanging out at David's apartment, I greeted
them with enthusiasm rather than shyness and diffidence.

At first I'd been disappointed when I heard voices in the hall giving away the fact that he already had guests. I'd turned up wearing only a shift dress and boots, no panties or underwear to get in the way of David's body. I'd been looking forward to whipping David's cock out of his fly and lowering myself on to it within seconds of arriving. But I crossed my legs and consoled myself that we'd make up for lost time when they all went home.

It was impossible to stay disappointed for long. The Collective welcomed me back as an old friend. I was now officially David's lover and he introduced me as such – 'girlfriend', he said, was too frivolous and mundane a word to describe the connection we had. Katya and Jem walked over and kissed me, held me tight in a lingering group hug. My body was alive to every touch, and their bodies pressed against mine sent a shiver down my spine that I hadn't been expecting.

There was a huge canvas stretched across the floor, a stiff sheet the size of two double beds. It surely must be the base for one of David's huge, wall-sized paintings. Although I loved his work, I'd been too busy with his dick to give any thought to his paintbrush.

'What are you working on?' I said brightly. 'One of these?' and I gestured towards the wall that was lined with panels of psychedelic, sensual swirls of colour.

'Ah,' said David, coming up behind me and putting

his arms around my waist. 'We've been wondering when you'd ask about them, haven't we?'

David's friends exchanged unreadable looks that unnerved me. I had the feeling everyone else was in on a secret that had been kept from me, and I didn't like it.

'These are a collective effort,' continued David. 'The efforts of The Collective. We . . . well . . . . we do them *together*. Do you want to see how?' He looked nervous, which was weird – I'd never seen him look anything but calm and in control.

'Sure,' I said. 'I want to know everything about you. I'd love to see you working on something so beautiful. But I didn't realise the rest of you were painters, too. Can anyone join in?' I asked, desperate not to be left out. 'Can I?'

'Yeah?' he said. 'Well . . . if you did, then it would be the best experience of my life. But why don't you wait and see how we do it first? Just watch to begin with. It might be a little soon for you.'

I was unnerved by the way David was talking in riddles. I watched, puzzled, as he strode across his apartment to a tall chest crammed full of paints. Rifling through his jumble of artist's materials, he settled on four huge jars of colour and massive brushes. I was so turned on watching the way his long legs covered such a distance so quickly, I didn't notice the movement behind me until a low, sensual moan made me turn around.

What I saw made me gasp. People undressed, slowly and sensually. I watched as Rosario peeled off her skin-tight white dress to reveal smooth, café-au-lait curves and magnificent, pendulous breasts. Jem and Louis tugged at each other's T-shirts. Katya displayed surprisingly feminine underwear underneath her drag-king suit: her mannish trousers discarded, she was naked but for a cute, pink floral bra. And David was unbuttoning his black shirt, unveiling the body that made me wet between the legs every time I saw it. Wearing only his jeans, he threw a few splashes of paint across the canvas: a slash of red, a vivid curl of orange, a bold streak of yellow, hot, warm colours on the cool, white space.

Katya was the first to tread on it and she lay back in the yellow paint, arching her back and spreading strong athletic legs to reveal a neatly trimmed black bush framing a glistening pink pussy. Within seconds, Louis was on her, kissing her, his brown back glistening as he scooped up a handful of red paint and smeared it across Katya's tits. He picked her up and rolled her across the canvas, creating the distinctive swirls that characterised David's work. Next, Jem joined their writhing bodies, crawling across the canvas on his hands and knees: Jem's hands were on Louis's back, trailing up and down, making his friend groan with pleasure. Rosario walked over to where Katya and Louis lay entwined and lay down next to Katya, who made a starfish with her hand and reached out to massage and lightly slap Rosario's breasts.

The assumptions I'd made their sexual preferences – that Jem and Katya were gay, and Louis was straight – vanished as they all devoured each other. Shock at my naivety turned to desire at the sight of all these beautiful people lost in a world of their own, painting with their bodies, the colours blending into one another, making magnificent pictures. Jem laid back while a blonde woman I didn't know took his impressive hard-on into her mouth and sucked greedily. Her knees slid on the slippery paint, legs spread as she tried to steady herself. Louis was behind her in a flash, whispering something in her ear and then, permission granted, eased his dick into her pussy, now plugged into the action. He held her by the waist and rocked gently, his hips rotating in time with the movement of her head. The noises were incredible: ten or eleven people moaning, whimpering, sighing and giggling, Katya's pussycat miaows contrasting with Louis's deep, baritone grunts of pleasure.

I couldn't believe what I was saw. Me, Charlie, a virgin only seven days ago, now witnessing an orgy and . . . I think . . . wanting to join in. Wanting to join in so badly it hurt. I had my hand between my legs, not touching my clit, but with the flat of my palm against my naked pussy, feeling it pulse and heat up, wondering if I dare to cross the line between spectator and participant. David came up behind me and put a hand on each shoulder, just as he had the first time he touched me.

'Well, well, Charlie-girl,' he said, hands travelling down to my breasts and making my knees buckle with longing for him. 'I think you like what you see, don't you? Would you like to join in?' I nodded, unable to speak, as he unzipped my shift dress letting it fall to the floor.

David held out his hand: I took it, stepped out of my puddled dress and let him lead me by the hand. He got to his knees, opened his arms and pulled me down on to the canvas. He moved as gently as though he were tucking me into a feather bed. 'Don't do anything you don't want to,' he said, as I felt warm paint tickle my back. 'I won't leave your side the whole time.'

I closed my eyes and let it happen: lips that I recognised as David's pressed themselves to my own parted mouth: I let him slip his tongue, familiar but thrilling, into my mouth and kiss me deeply. His body was pressed against my side and he slid his hand between my legs. Another pair of lips, so soft and smooth that they had to be female, wrapped themselves around my nipple: two soft, large breasts resting on my stomach told me that this must be Rosario. I opened my eyes to see the corkscrew curls of her hair trailing over my breasts and shoulders, tickling the thin receptive skin there. She was soft, gentle and sensitive, kissing, sucking, licking my breast in a way that encouraged gentle lapping waves of desire quite different to the roaring fires of lust David usually kindled in me – but equally delicious.

Meanwhile David went to work between my legs. He slid two, three, then four fingers in and out of me. He knew my body's responses better than I did: within seconds my whole frame jack-knifed, a sure sign that an over-powering climax would not be far away.

I turned my head to one side and watched the group of bodies writhing an arm's length away. They were so close I could smell their individual musk, natural fragrances mingling with scented oils, shampoos and perfumes. I didn't need to join in: the sights, sounds and smells were enough to turn me on. A hand reached out and pulled Rosario away from me, and she disappeared into the throng. I lay beside David transfixed by the performance in front of us.

One by one, The Collective hit their climax, their moans of satisfaction making a continuous hum that echoed throughout the apartment. Rosario was the last one to reach orgasm, Louis bringing her off with his tongue. Sated, The Collective lay in a tangled heap for just long enough to get their breath back, then leapt up and headed for David's bijou bathroom, giggling as they went.

David helped me to my feet. The canvas lay before me, a glorious, flaming mess of blazing colours like a giant bonfire.

'It's beautiful,' I said, and it was.

'It's not quite finished yet,' said David. He got up, his lean body streaked with flame-coloured marbling and fetched a final tin of paint. 'This is for you. I've saved this for you. For us,' and he poured bright, glittering gold liquid all over my arse and back: I gasped as the cold liquid chilled my skin. I lay down on the canvas sending splashes of metallic pigment everywhere, David watching me, cock in his hand. The sight of his erection – the only part of his body not covered in paint – made me want him inside me.

I knelt on all fours and raised my arse. He was inside me immediately, his dick hotter and harder than I'd ever felt it before. I squeezed my legs together and rocked my way to an orgasm that ripped through me like lightning. David came at the same time, his balls slapping against my thighs and arse as his orgasm jolted his whole body. We let our come drip down my legs and fleck the paint below. Only we would ever know it was there.

In the bathroom the rest of The Collective towelled themselves off, glowing and exhausted by their art experience. Katya and Rosario were washing each other down in the old-fashioned roll-top bath: although not exactly built for four people they made room for me and David to step in and get under the hot jet of water from the showerhead in Katya's hand. Rosario shampooed the paint from my hair and gently, tenderly rinsed the bright oil colours and semen from my pounded pussy. David let her soap between his arse and under his dick and lather up his balls. He didn't take his eyes off me the whole time. There was no room for jealousy here: Rosario might have David's dick in her hand, but I had his heart and his mind.

When we'd scrubbed ourselves clean, we wrapped ourselves in towels and settled in on the window seat where we'd shared our first kiss. The Collective were curled up in pairs and threesomes on the sofa, idly and affectionately stroking each other's hair. The masterpiece was now complete: the gold paint brought the whole thing to life, so that it seemed to flicker and glow like a giant fireball. My metallic handprints and the impression from our knees where David had taken me from behind danced and caught the light like sparks.

'I'll call it '*Dancer's Inferno*',' he said. 'You were amazing tonight. It is my privilege to take you on this journey.' He bit lightly on my ear, igniting a fresh shiver of desire. 'And Charlie-girl? I promise you, the best is yet to come.' I smiled, stretched my body and purred like a cat, thinking of all tomorrow's parties.

WATERBABY

This taboo-busting confession came from an innocent-looking blonde in her late twenties. It's all the more erotic for the contrast between her demure appearance and her depraved behaviour. But her story proves that when you push boundaries, a sexual experience you imagined to be off-limits can be just the adventure you were looking for. Not for the faint-hearted.

Greg had been part of my crowd for years. There were twelve of us. We'd been at college together and gone from a tribe of scruffy teenagers staying awake for whole week-ends to successful twenty-somethings who'd regularly take over the leather sofas in the pub on Sunday afternoons. In the ten years we'd hung out, through jobs, through uni, Greg had always been there, in the background. Always there, but no one really knew him. He didn't say much, but then boys as attractive as he didn't have to. He looked like a dark David Beckham, his chestnut brown hair that he re-styled every week, the firmest, cleanest profile you'd ever seen, and not an strand of hair on his lightly tanned body. His clothes were always immaculate.

Our male friends would dread introducing their girl-friends to Greg. Women's jaws would drop as they met him for the first time. You could see them mentally strip-ping him: knowing that underneath his smart, expensive clothes there was a classically sculpted body, lean torso and perfect six-pack stomach. On first sight, he was breath-taking. But after a while, you'd become accustomed to Greg and his charmed looks. And a little while after that, you'd kinda grow bored by him. All the sexy jawlines in the world don't count for much if there's no conversation. The truth was, that although most of us had experimented with one another – from college bed-hopping to one-night stands in our new London life – Greg had never really been involved with any of us. The few girlfriends he'd had were, of course, beautiful, but had tended not to stick around for more than two or three dates. When we did speculate about Greg's sexuality – which wasn't that often to be honest because, looks aside, he was unremarkable – we just assumed he was gay, and waiting for the right moment to come out of the closet.

One night I came to realise that Greg was *anything* but gay. It was a Saturday night, at a new bar in our corner of North London. It was Sheila's thirtieth birthday and instead of the usual jeans-T-shirts-and-pub routine, we all made an effort and were dressed up to sink plenty of cock-tails somewhere fabulous. It was a balmy July evening during the hottest summer of our young lives and we all wore as little clothing as was decent. I'd had a long, luxurious shower in my en suite wetroom: shaved my legs and rubbed scented body oil into my skin. By the time I dressed I was so hot and sticky, I needed another shower. It was that kind of summer.

I checked myself out in my full-length mirror before leaving the house. My blue top that looked like a silk scarf (and wasn't much bigger) showed just the right amount of flesh. Could I get away without wearing a bra? I examined myself from every angle before deciding it was too hot for underwear anyway. And, yeah, I could get away with it. My tits were round and high and had an all-over tan from sunbathing topless in the back garden. I finished the outfit with a denim mini and silver slingbacks. It was too humid to bother straightening my blonde hair, so I'd left it to dry naturally, and piled the resulting messy curls on top of my head, leaving a few strands to frame my face. As an afterthought, I put on a pair of long silver and sapphire earrings which brushed my collar bone and caressed the soft, sensitive flesh of my neck.

'Wow,' gasped Sheila and whistled when she picked me up in the taxi. 'You're going to be fighting off the boys tonight!' I hoped she was right. To be frank, it had been a while since I'd had a really good fuck. None of the boyfriends I'd had in the last year or so had delivered in the bedroom department: they'd been keen but cautious, and I was ready for some serious fun. Here, I was definitely in my comfort zone – same mates, same job, same flat. I wanted to recapture the feeling I had at eighteen – that anything was possible. I needed to find a man who'd make me fall back in love (or lust?) with sex. And I wanted to meet that man tonight.

The bar had only been open a couple of weeks, and it was packed. Scantily clad bodies were crowded into the tiny space, strangers touching each other's warm flesh and not having to apologise. There was no air conditioning. That didn't bother me though: the tacky skin of other bodies released horny pheromones, newly showered and perfumed bodies mingling with fresh sweat. The air was ripe with the musky aroma of sexual possibility. The place had dark-red walls and black chandeliers, and huge, antique-effect Louis XIV mirrors. They reflected sexy, dusky versions of ourselves back at us. The whole venue looked like some period-piece brothel but it was pretty sexy. I caught sight of myself in a mirror as I queued for the bar. I look good, I thought. Tonight could be the night, and I scanned the length of the bar for a handsome stranger to whisk me away and ravish me. Instead, I saw Greg, looking handsome and fresh in a crisp, light blue shirt, open to the chest, a chunky silver necklace round his neck. I nodded a hello then turned my attention back to the barman.

I didn't want risk a hangover, so I ordered a glass of water with my cocktail. It was so hot, I made sure that I chased every drink with something non-alcoholic. An hour or two into the evening, I'd given up looking for Prince Charming and decided to concentrate on my friends instead. A couple of times I'd noticed that Greg was watching me more intensely than usual, especially when I was drinking. When he got up to go to the bar, he offered to buy me another. 'Thanks,' I said. 'It's too hot for another cocktail. Just get me a long drink of something soft, please.'

He came back with a jug of iced water and a single glass, which he poured out and held to my lips. 'Drink it,' he said, and that intensity I'd noticed before was back. If he hadn't been so good-looking, it would have been creepy. As soon as I'd finished, he poured me another one and offered it to me.

'No thanks Greg – I'll be on the loo all night as it is,' I said. At that his face lit up and he licked his lips. What an odd boy he is, I thought. But the look in his face made his features come alive, and I was reminded how horny I'd thought he was the very first time I'd seen him.

It wasn't long before I really did need the loo. I made

my way across the room to the ladies. The toilets were fashionably unisex, and were tucked away in a dark corner of the club. Great. One toilet for a million people – and the queue was already five deep. Why hadn't I gone before? My heart sank when two girls disappeared into the cubicle at once. They'd be in there for hours, chatting about fellas and re-touching their lipgloss. I crossed my legs, tried not to wince and slid my mini down so that it hung off my hips and didn't put any extra pressure on my bladder. Then I felt a presence behind me. I turned around and it was Greg: I could just about make out his features in the dark red light of the club.

'When you've got to go . . .' I said, not wanting to make small talk as all my energies were concentrated on holding it in.

'Yes, but think of how good it'll be when you *do*,' said Greg in a husky voice that wasn't his usual tone. 'It'll feel like an orgasm. Deferred gratification is always preferable to getting what you want right away. It's the build-up that makes it so exciting.' Geez, in all the time I'd known him, this was the longest sentence I'd ever heard Greg speak, and to top it off, it was also the weirdest, which was rather distracting as I jigged on one foot, legs crossed. But there was something about the urgency in his voice that strangely turned me on. I had never thought of pissing as compar-able to an orgasm before, but now that I imagined the sweet relief of relaxing and letting it go, the agony I was in seemed even worse. Greg's words prompted a chain of thoughts that, to my surprise, led to a heaviness between my legs and the beginnings of a wetness that had nothing to do with wanting the bathroom. Great. I now had a throbbing clit to contend with as well as a desperate need to piss. What was Greg playing at?

He answered my unspoken question by inching forward so that his chin was resting on the top of my head and – was that a hard-on I could feel in the small of my back? No, it couldn't be. Still, the thought of his smooth brown cock made me feel even more uncomfortable. The pressure on my bladder, now exacerbated by an aroused clitoris, was making me more and more uneasy.

'Ohh,' said Greg, in his new voice. 'Don't be embarrassed. Let it go.' And then, so quickly I had no time to protest, he slid his hand down the waistband of my skirt and pressed, hard, on my bladder. It was a feat of immense willpower that I managed not to piss myself right there in the club. Too shocked to move, I let him press the heel of his hand down there while his fingers slid expertly down to my clit, massaging through my thin lace thong, which was already soaking. My clit responded in seconds. I let out an involuntary moan of pleasure as well as pain.

He went to work on me then, index and ring fingers making minute circles either side of my clit, middle finger tracing my lips, and that hand pressing down on my bladder. It would have been so easy to come, but I knew that if I did, I'd wet myself in the middle of a club. No orgasm was worth that kind of humiliation . . . was it? My eyes were hazy and half-closed, but in the dim light I saw the two girls leave the cubicle and the next woman enter. I was now first in the queue, and it was so dark that surely Greg would slip in with me and finish what he'd started. The knowledge that I would soon be able to release this agonising but exquisite tension meant I could exercise mind over matter and hold on for a couple of minutes longer.

His voice in my ear was eager, insistent. 'I can't wait to lick my fingers when I'm done with you.' So this was what made Greg tick. I'd wanted a sexual adventure, but would this be a case of 'be careful what you wish for'? I wasn't sure I was ready for something as dark and kinky as this. But I couldn't deny that it felt good, probably purely because it ought not to. Dizzy with the need to relieve myself, I leaned back on Greg's body to steady myself. His cock, rock-hard, was straining the crotch of his jeans. No doubting whether he had a hard-on: he was solid, even more turned on than I was. Greg sighed as I pushed my hips against his erection and he lowered his voice to a whisper.

'Of course, for the ultimate release of tension, you can piss and come at the same time. Guys can't do that.

But we can make you do it. Have *you* ever pissed and come at the same time? Have you? Would you like to?' His voice was urgent, rasping.

His free hand wandered around to the back of my tiny skirt and he slipped three fingers into my aching pussy, stretching it, filling me up and making me feel as though I was about to burst. The once-dull ache in my lower abdomen developed into acute pain. I bit my lip to fight back the tears of pain and frustration. I didn't want Greg to stop, but I wasn't sure how long I could hold on for. I could feel his thumb pushing aside the lace of the back of my thong, and I knew that the next thing he did would be to slide it up my arsehole. If he did that, I'd feel so overwhelmed, so replete, that I'd have gone past the point of no return. No way could I let that happen, no matter how good it felt. I was just about to remove Greg's hand when the bathroom door opened. Thank God, we were free to go in. I could let go – lose control – of *all* my body.

In considerable discomfort I walked forward. Greg moved with me, still with both of his hands inside my panties. The bathroom was opulent, black-tiled and lit only by one onyx candelabra. In the flickering light I could see how erect my nipples were, poking through my blue top: at last, now we have some privacy. Now Greg could touch them. When I was this close to coming, a flick on a nipple could tip me over the edge into a climax. At this stage, so what if I wet myself: I couldn't work out whether the need to orgasm or the need to piss was more overwhelming. I turned to say this to Greg. But at that moment whipped his hands out of my panties, pushed me forward so that I staggered into the bathroom and pulled the door shut behind me. I think I heard him whisper, 'Next time,' before I found myself alone, turned on, more than a little confused, but above all, desperate for the bathroom.

I didn't have time to open the door and run after him: I had to sit down on the toilet and let it all go, finally releasing the tension my whole pelvis had held on to for the last hour or so. Greg was right. It *was* like an orgasm, a massive orgasm. I could feel every muscle in my body melt and the stream of golden liquid soothed and calmed my throbbing pussy. I thought it would never end, but when the stream had finished, I sat there in the half-lit stall. I may have satisfied one primal urge, but another pressing need remained unfulfilled. I didn't need to think twice: my hand was between my legs, pinching my clitoris, rubbing it provided the rapid stimulation I needed to finish what Greg had started. I came in seconds, detonating like a timebomb that had been ticking for years.

I splashed water on my face and looked at myself in the mirror. My eyes glittered and my face was flushed. I reapplied my lip gloss. I rearranged my top so that the fabric was extra tight across my still-erect nipples. I wanted Greg to see what he'd just missed. I went out to finding search of him at the bar, intending to tell him off, hoping he'd come home with me.

Instead of Greg, I saw Sheila. 'Darling!' she said, flushed and happy on her birthday champagne. 'A few of us are going to a club. You coming?'

'Oh,' I said, looking for Greg over her shoulder. 'Who's going along?'

'Well, Greg's disappeared off home so it's just the eight of us. Come on! But don't worry, it's not like he contributes much anyway. It'll be fun!'

My mind was reeling. Why had Greg got me stoked up like that only to abandon me at the crucial moment? Knowing I wouldn't have him that night made me want him even more. The taxi ride to the club took us over cobbled streets: as the vibrations from the vehicle travelled through my pelvis, I was astonished to find myself becoming aroused for the second time that evening – and once I'd had an orgasm, it was usually a good couple of days before that unmistakeable tension would start to build and swell again. We piled into the club and on to the dance floor. I wasn't really feeling the music that night, but I *was* aware that I was attracting a lot of male attention. I toyed with the idea of taking one of them home, to satisfy my burgeoning lust, but it was Greg, Greg and his fucked-up mind games that I really wanted. At 2 a.m., I made my apologies to Sheila and hailed a cab home.

The night was sweltering, and although I lay naked on top of the sheets, I couldn't get comfortable. Sleep was out of the question. Every time I closed my eyes, I saw Greg's face, replayed our conversation. I fantasised that he had stayed with me in that bathroom, that I'd let him bring me to orgasm, that I'd let go – really let go. I began to shiver with desire despite the heat. At 4 a.m., I was as horny as when Greg had been standing behind me with his massive hard-on prodding my back. I padded across my bedroom and took my vibrator out of its hiding place in the wardrobe. I lay on the bed, holding it against my clit. In two minutes, I experienced another orgasm, gentler than the first. It was the sleeping pill I needed. I drifted off to sleep as the sun came up, my vibrator lying beside me on my bed.

I woke up around midday, to the sound of a persistent beeping noise which told me that I had an unanswered text message on my phone. I fumbled for my mobile in my handbag by my bed, and as I saw the vibe lying next to me on the pillow, the confusion and the sexual high of last night came flooding back. I had finally worked out what made Greg tick. I could confidently report back to the group that he was *not* gay. But could I tell them how I found out? Already, the curious, highly charged experience we'd shared felt like a secret no one but Greg would even begin to understand.

The text message was from him. It was nothing if not to the point.

'Fancy a drink?' it said.

I never wanted another drink in my life: I still had my make-up on and could still taste last night's champagne in my otherwise dry mouth. But I had to see Greg again, find out if last night was just a weird one-off or the start of something incredible. I texted back: 'Sure, why not?'

I needed a shower. Wrapping myself in a towel, I walked into my wetroom. Brushing my teeth woke me up. I stood under the shower lathering up my favourite scented shower gel. I took a piss standing up in the shower, thinking about how it felt. No more or less enjoyable than going to the bathroom ever was. I shook my head. This was madness. Was I ever going to have normal bodily functions again without getting horny and thinking about Greg?

I towelled myself off and was applying body lotion to my legs when the doorbell rang. I huffed downstairs, cursing the tiny letterbox that meant I had to open the door every day to get anything bigger than a postcard.

It was Greg. Beads of sweat stood out on his brow and upper lip, and his hair was damp, curling a little around his neck. He wore cut-off jeans and a white T-shirt which outlined his pecs and made his tan stand out. And he carried two massive take-away colas from a fast food restaurant – the huge, bucket-sized cups you see in America.

'Hello you,' he said. He wore the same hungry, serious look I'd seen on his face last night.

'Hello you,' I said, suddenly shy and embarrassed and very conscious of being naked under my towel.

'I thought about you all night,' he said.

This suddenly seemed like a very odd conversation to be having on my doorstep on a Sunday morning, with the passengers of London buses staring at me in my towel. 'I guess you'd better come in,' I said. 'Wait in the living room.'

I left Greg and his drinks in the lounge and dashed into my bedroom, where I pulled on a vest and pink cotton hotpants. I didn't bother with underwear – it was hot already and I wanted to get dressed as quickly as possible.

I came back in to find him still sitting there, eyes fixed on me. I sat down on the sofa next to him.

'I thought about you all night,' he said again.

'Yeah . . .' I admitted. 'I kind of wondered what had happened to you.' And then I thought, I might as well come out with it, 'I was rather under the impression you'd be coming in the bathroom with me to finish what you'd started.'

'Last night was just the beginning,' he said. 'A kind

of test, if you like.' I couldn't think of anything to say, so I let him keep talking.

'You must know I've been crazy about you for years,' he continued. I stared at him. How could I know that, when he'd never said more than six words to me since college? 'But I need someone who can be a partner with me in my sexual world. And that was a test to see if you were strong enough.'

My mind was reeling. My first reaction was: this guy's kinky, he's too intense, you could be getting in over your head. End it now before you do something you regret. My second reaction was physical, not mental. My lips parted, and I caught my breath as I thought of what it was Greg wanted to do with me and how bad it would be – and how good that would feel. I leaned forward on the sofa, tilting my face up to his, closing my eyes and waiting for his kiss. But instead of pressing his lips to mine, he pushed the cola drink into my hand.

'Why don't you have a drink first?' he said. Then I knew that sleeping with Greg would be very different from going to bed with any other new lover I'd ever had. I could either refuse to drink up and ask him to have straight sex, nothing kinky. Or I could play his game, and get drawn into his depraved little world. Again, my body made the choice for me: I had wrapped my lips around the straw and started sucking greedily before my mind had made a conscious decision otherwise. I downed maybe a litre of liquid in thirty seconds: some of it dribbled down my chin and along my neck. Greg's tongue was there immediately, licking me clean, sketching wet spirals on my neck and breasts. After I'd gulped the second long drink, I was gasping for breath. Greg didn't give me a chance to come up for air: his lips were locked on mine. He lay on top of me, lavishing slow, luxurious kisses on me, turning me on more subtly than any clit massage ever could.

After a few minutes, we pulled apart. Greg placed the palm of his hand on my lower abdomen, pressed hard and raised one eyebrow. I shook my head, answering his unspoken question: I didn't need to go yet. He disappeared to the kitchen and returned with a glass jug of water.

'I don't think you're full enough yet,' he whispered. 'And I want you full before I fuck you.'

The word 'fuck' spoken by Greg made me gasp with excitement. And with that he held back my hair and forced the jug lip to my own lips, holding my nose so that I had to open my mouth. I had no choice but to gulp it back. Again, I spilled as much as I drank: the cold water made my skimpy white vest stick to my skin, creating goosebumps and waking up my nipples despite the humid atmosphere. Greg ran one hand along the dripping, clinging cotton. It was obvious I wore no underwear. I saw Greg's eyes trace the contours of my breasts and belly through the now translucent fabric: his naked desire fuelled my own and I felt the heat rush to my restless pussy. I moaned with pleasure.

He peeled off my damp vest, exposing tits that sat up and begged for his attention. True to his principle of deferred gratification, he didn't satisfy them with a caress or a kiss: instead he rolled down my hotpants, pulled them over my ankles. A little damp patch was evidence of how turned on I was. He closed his eyes and held the hotpants to his nose, inhaling deeply. I lay there, naked and watched him take in my scent. Through his open shirt I could see a rock-hard stomach and a line of light brown hair, tapering into an arrow pointing towards his dick. God, he was beautiful. And he wanted me.

Greg let the hotpants fall to the floor and opened his eyes. Watching me, he unfastened the single button on his white shirt and shrugged it off his shoulders, revealing a torso even more sculpted and bronzed than I'd imagined. Then it was time for him to remove his shorts: his tight, muscled hips flanked a dick every bit as beautiful as the rest of him: his light brown pubic hair was cropped into a neat rectangle, all the better to show off smooth, even balls and a thick, sturdy erection. A powerful throb convulsed my pussy and I felt a drop of juice emerge: I spread my legs, showing Greg I was ready to have him inside me.

But instead of climbing on top of me, he knelt between my legs and slid a pink, silky tongue between my lips.

'So pink,' he said. 'So wet. So beautiful.' As his tongue traced the contours of my cunt and I felt the pressure mount, another feeling crept up on me.

'Greg,' I whispered, 'I'm getting full. I need to go.'

'Not yet you don't,' he said, and turned his attention to my clitoris. His tongue swept around it, coming tantalisingly close but never quite providing the direct stimulation I needed. His hands reached for my nipples and twisted them, pulling my tits out to the side, then down, a sweet agony that made me cry out in pleasure or pain, I couldn't tell which any more. He continued his torment by pressing his forehead on my lower abdomen, making my need to go to the bathroom more urgent. He looked up from his cruel tease.

'What do you want most? To come or to pee?' He said, his beautiful face hovering over mine, smooth brown cock upright between his thighs.

'I want to do both . . . I need both . . . please let me . . .' I said, tossing my head from side to side in frustration.

'Well, you're lucky. You do get to do both. But not until I say so.'

And with that he picked me up from where I lay on the armchair and carried me to the wetroom. Grateful for a break from the pressure in my pelvis, I wrapped my legs around him. My pussy was pressed against his navel. I could feel the hair on his belly tickle my clit, and the tip of his dick jabbed at the sensitive inch of skin between my pussy and arsehole. It was the first time I'd been in contact with his dick and I had to fight the urge to lower myself down on to it, to force him inside me. But he'd said not yet. Not yet. So I kissed him, working my way around his teeth with my tongue. He kissed me back, urgently, his tongue making tiny thrusts towards the back of my throat. When he lay me down on the mosaic floor of the wetroom, I could see the silver trail my pussy juice had made on the skin of his taut stomach.

He ran the tap. 'Oldest trick in the book,' he said, smiling. 'It'll make you need to go so bad you won't be able to hold it in.' The smile vanished. 'You're not allowed to go yet, of course. But I am. Spread your legs. You're soaking,' he said. 'But I think you could get a little wetter.'

I was shocked into silence as he relieved himself between my parted legs. But the feel-good factor quickly outstripped any hang-ups I had about breaking this, the ultimate taboo. Oh, who am I kidding? The taboo was half the turn on. The drip-drip-drip of his golden liquid, the colour of champagne, teased my clit in a way no fingers, tongues or toy ever had. I wanted more. 'Faster! Harder!' I screamed. He let go then, unleashing a torrent on to me. Because of his erection, he had to use his hand to direct the flow, like a fireman controlling a hose. When he'd finished, his hard-on looked thicker and harder than before.

'It's nearly your turn,' he murmured, kneeling over me on the floor. With a sudden violence, he pressed hard on my lower abdomen. A tiny droplet of urine leaked out. I couldn't help it.

'Control yourself!' shouted Greg, and his voice was so stern I froze, clenched my whole pelvis, tried to stem the flow. 'Not until I say so,' he said, straddling my body. A single droplet of piss glistened on the end of his hard-on. 'Do you understand?' I nodded, and suddenly he was inside me. My cunt closed around his dick as hard as a clamshell, but I didn't dare to relax, even as that beautiful body moved up and down, backwards and forwards above mine.

Seconds before I was about to cave in, Greg looked down at me and mouthed the word 'now'. At the same time he slid his hand between us and took my swollen, frustrated clitoris between his thumb and forefinger and pinched hard: I let go, in all senses of the word. Relief overwhelmed shame as violent spasms jerked my entire body. I came hard, losing control over every bodily function. At the sight of the puddle that spread around us, Greg came too, his hot, salty spunk mingling with my own water.

We lay on the floor of my wetroom together. Greg's hard-on subsided inside me and we breathed each other's breath, our heartbeats returning to normal. After a couple of minutes, he pulled me to my feet and led me underneath the showerhead. I turned on the tap. The hot, steaming water brought my mind back into focus. I'd just had the most intense, powerful sexual encounter of my life. And by far the darkest. But I felt no guilt or shame, just a feeling of satisfaction deeper than any I'd experienced before.

Greg was inches away from my face, lathering bodywash between his hands. 'I bet you didn't know you had that in you,' he said, a smile that was nearly a smirk on his lips. 'But I did. I've been waiting years to do that with you, my waterbaby.'

I closed my eyes and relaxed as Greg began to wash between my legs. I guess we all have it in us. It just takes a close encounter with the right person to unleash a spine-tingling side to your sexuality you never knew you possessed. And who knows where you'll find him! My advice? Accept a date with that quiet guy at work. Get to know that mysterious man who's fascinated you for years. Give him a chance. You might just find the adventure you were looking for.